Walt Disney's

Donald Duck

Executive Editor: Gary Groth

Senior Editor: J. Michael Catron

Colorist: Rich Tommaso

Cover Colorist: Keeli McCarthy

Designer: Keeli McCarthy

Production: Paul Baresh

Associate Publisher: Eric Reynolds

Publisher: Gary Groth

Fantagraphics Books, Inc.
7563 Lake City Way NE
Seattle, WA 98115

2015-08 Casa Blanca Comics 8-

For a free catalog of more books like this, classic comic book and newspaper strip collections, and other fine works of artistry, call (800) 657-1100 or visit fantagraphics.com. Follow us on Twitter at @fantagraphics and on Facebook at facebook.com/fantagraphics.

ISBN 978-1-60699-820-5

Printed in Malaysia

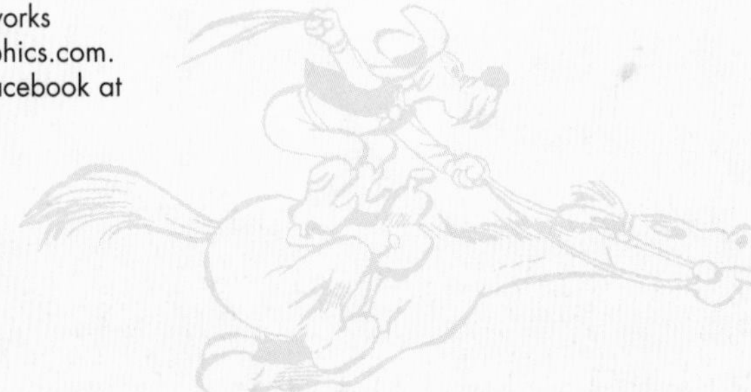

SHERIFF *of* BULLET VALLEY

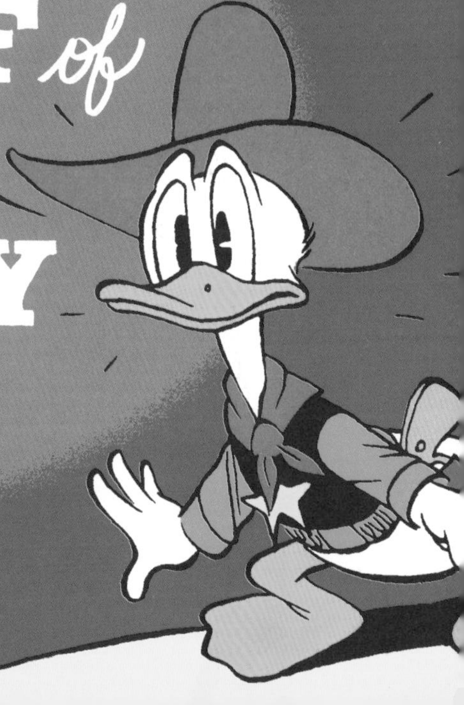

FANTAGRAPHICS BOOKS

CONTENTS

ALL STORIES WRITTEN AND DRAWN BY CARL BARKS

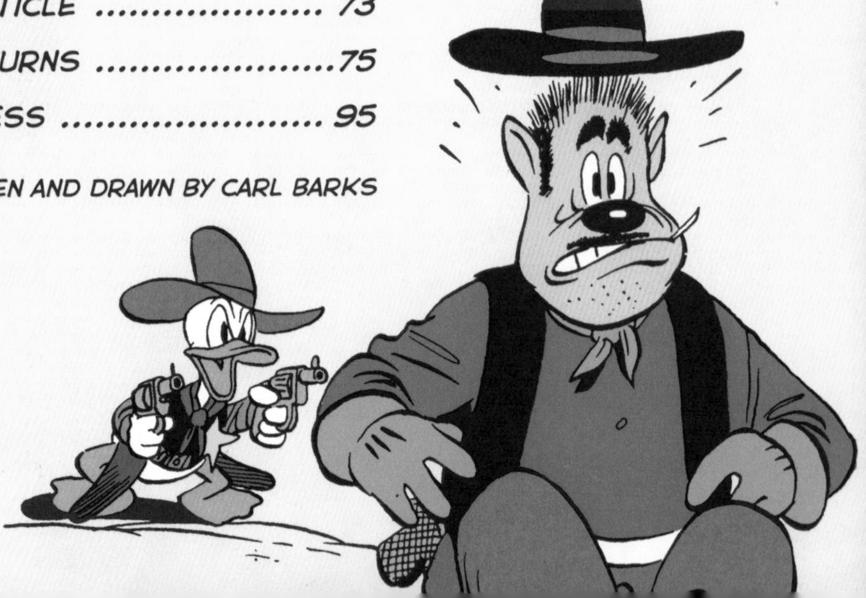

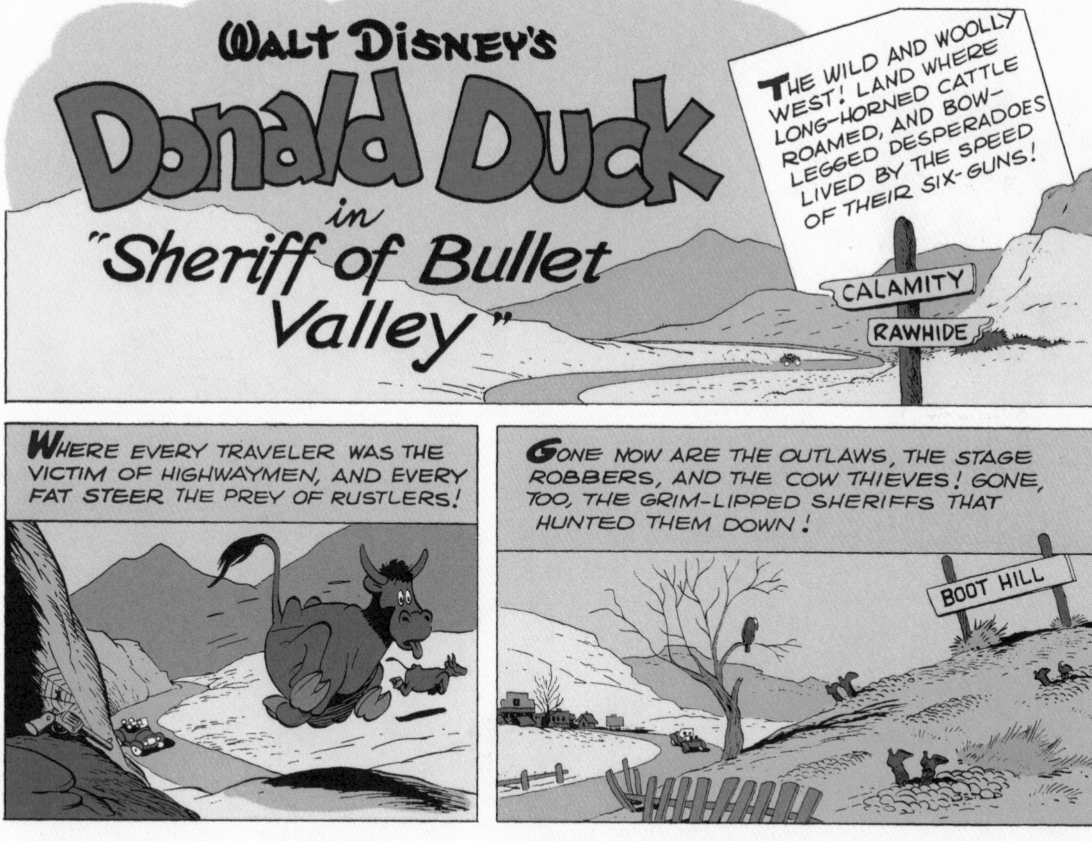
WALT DISNEY'S
Donald Duck
in
"Sheriff of Bullet Valley"
THE WILD AND WOOLLY WEST! LAND WHERE LONG-HORNED CATTLE ROAMED, AND BOW-LEGGED DESPERADOES LIVED BY THE SPEED OF THEIR SIX-GUNS!
CALAMITY
RAWHIDE
WHERE EVERY TRAVELER WAS THE VICTIM OF HIGHWAYMEN, AND EVERY FAT STEER THE PREY OF RUSTLERS!
GONE NOW ARE THE OUTLAWS, THE STAGE ROBBERS, AND THE COW THIEVES! GONE, TOO, THE GRIM-LIPPED SHERIFFS THAT HUNTED THEM DOWN!
BOOT HILL

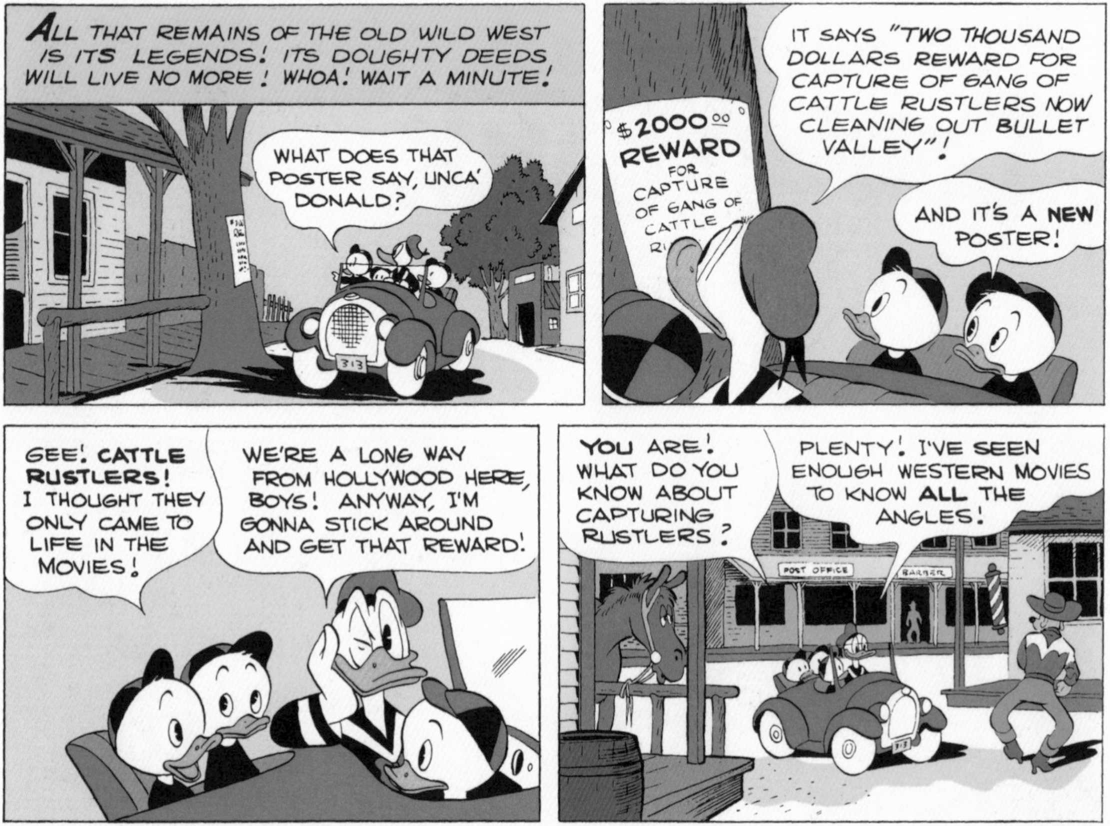
ALL THAT REMAINS OF THE OLD WILD WEST IS ITS LEGENDS! ITS DOUGHTY DEEDS WILL LIVE NO MORE! WHOA! WAIT A MINUTE!
WHAT DOES THAT POSTER SAY, UNCA' DONALD?
313
IT SAYS "TWO THOUSAND DOLLARS REWARD FOR CAPTURE OF GANG OF CATTLE RUSTLERS NOW CLEANING OUT BULLET VALLEY"!
$2000.00 REWARD FOR CAPTURE OF GANG OF CATTLE
AND IT'S A NEW POSTER!
GEE! CATTLE RUSTLERS! I THOUGHT THEY ONLY CAME TO LIFE IN THE MOVIES!
WE'RE A LONG WAY FROM HOLLYWOOD HERE, BOYS! ANYWAY, I'M GONNA STICK AROUND AND GET THAT REWARD!
YOU ARE! WHAT DO YOU KNOW ABOUT CAPTURING RUSTLERS?
PLENTY! I'VE SEEN ENOUGH WESTERN MOVIES TO KNOW ALL THE ANGLES!
POST OFFICE
BARBER

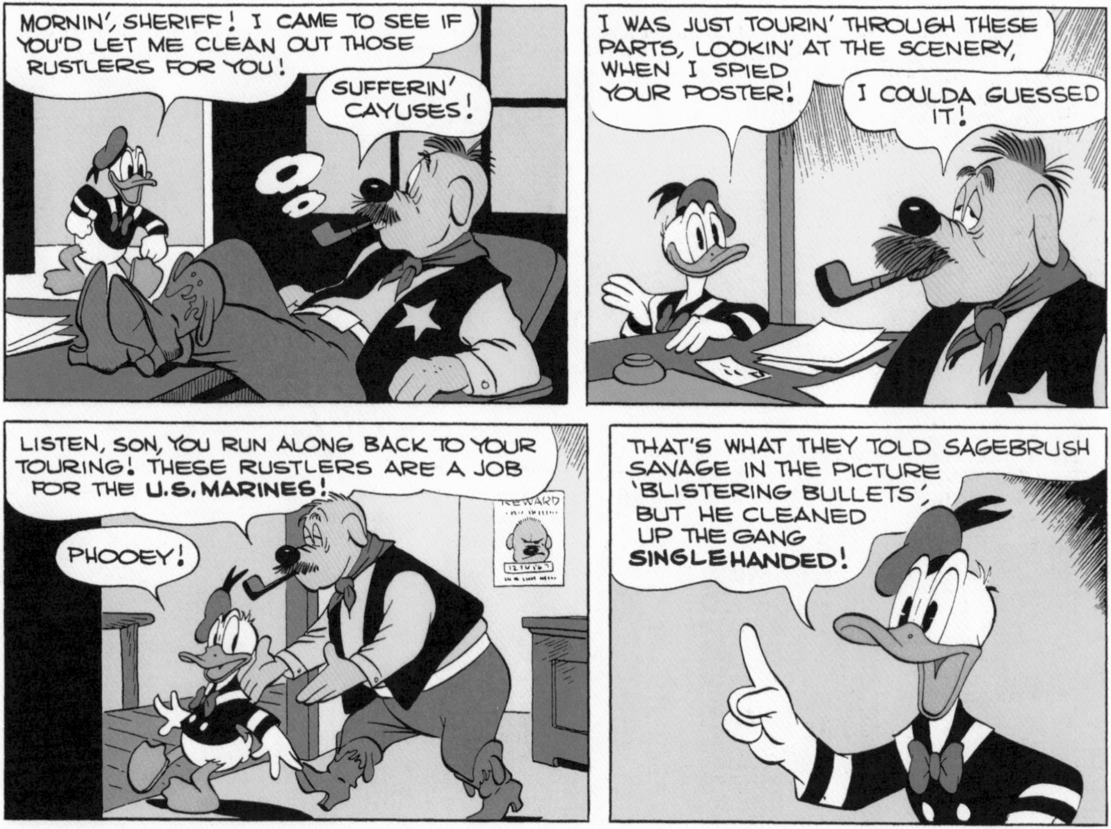
MORNIN', SHERIFF! I CAME TO SEE IF YOU'D LET ME CLEAN OUT THOSE RUSTLERS FOR YOU!
SUFFERIN' CAYUSES!
I WAS JUST TOURIN' THROUGH THESE PARTS, LOOKIN' AT THE SCENERY, WHEN I SPIED YOUR POSTER!
I COULDA GUESSED IT!
LISTEN, SON, YOU RUN ALONG BACK TO YOUR TOURING! THESE RUSTLERS ARE A JOB FOR THE **U.S. MARINES**!
PHOOEY!
THAT'S WHAT THEY TOLD SAGEBRUSH SAVAGE IN THE PICTURE 'BLISTERING BULLETS', BUT HE CLEANED UP THE GANG **SINGLEHANDED**!

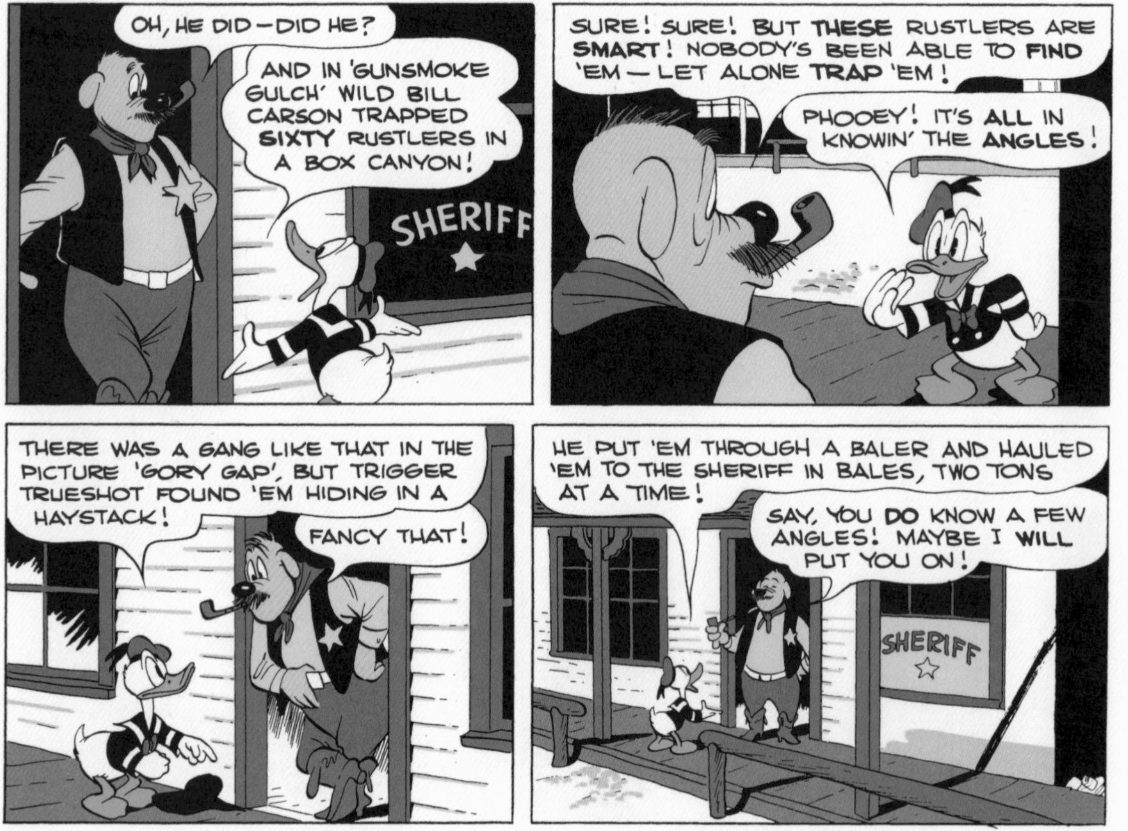
OH, HE DID—DID HE?
AND IN 'GUNSMOKE GULCH' WILD BILL CARSON TRAPPED SIXTY RUSTLERS IN A BOX CANYON!
SHERIFF
SURE! SURE! BUT THESE RUSTLERS ARE SMART! NOBODY'S BEEN ABLE TO FIND 'EM — LET ALONE TRAP 'EM!
PHOOEY! IT'S ALL IN KNOWIN' THE ANGLES!
THERE WAS A GANG LIKE THAT IN THE PICTURE 'GORY GAP', BUT TRIGGER TRUESHOT FOUND 'EM HIDING IN A HAYSTACK!
FANCY THAT!
HE PUT 'EM THROUGH A BALER AND HAULED 'EM TO THE SHERIFF IN BALES, TWO TONS AT A TIME!
SAY, YOU DO KNOW A FEW ANGLES! MAYBE I WILL PUT YOU ON!
SHERIFF

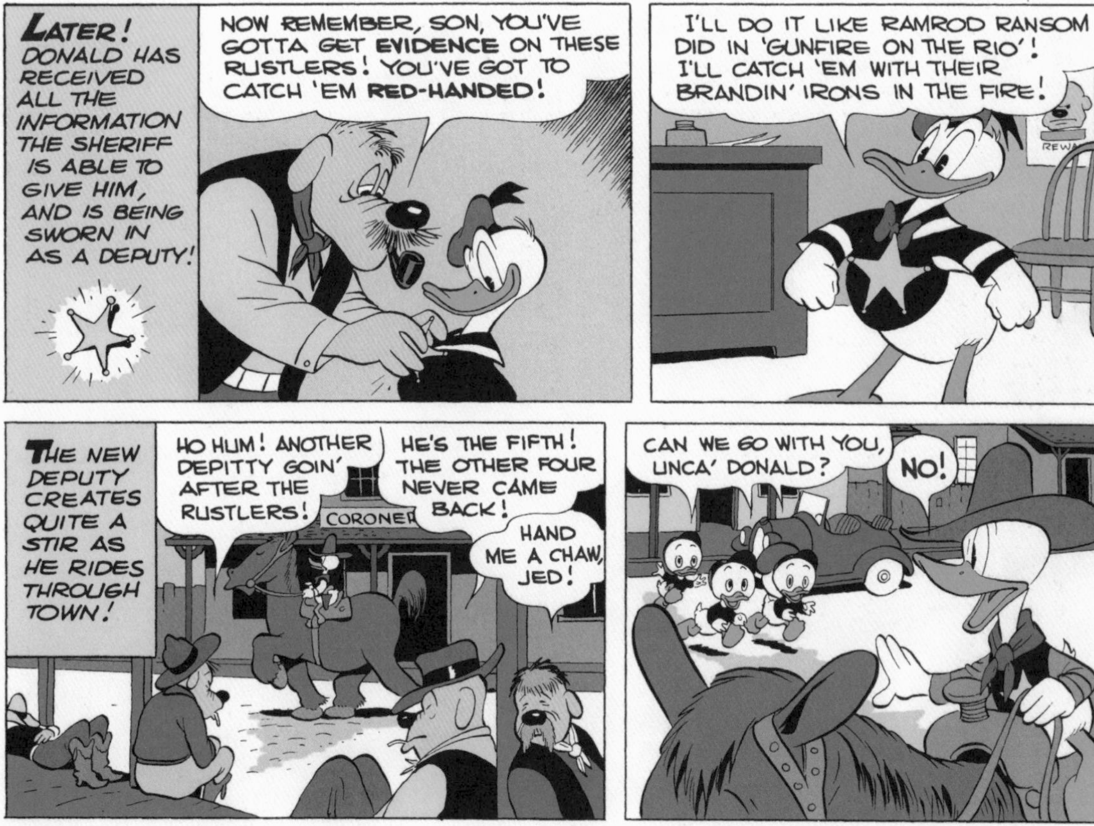
LATER! DONALD HAS RECEIVED ALL THE INFORMATION THE SHERIFF IS ABLE TO GIVE HIM, AND IS BEING SWORN IN AS A DEPUTY!
NOW REMEMBER, SON, YOU'VE GOTTA GET EVIDENCE ON THESE RUSTLERS! YOU'VE GOT TO CATCH 'EM RED-HANDED!
I'LL DO IT LIKE RAMROD RANSOM DID IN 'GUNFIRE ON THE RIO'! I'LL CATCH 'EM WITH THEIR BRANDIN' IRONS IN THE FIRE!
REWA
THE NEW DEPUTY CREATES QUITE A STIR AS HE RIDES THROUGH TOWN!
HO HUM! ANOTHER DEPITTY GOIN' AFTER THE RUSTLERS!
HE'S THE FIFTH! THE OTHER FOUR NEVER CAME BACK!
CORONER
HAND ME A CHAW, JED!
CAN WE GO WITH YOU, UNCA' DONALD?
NO!

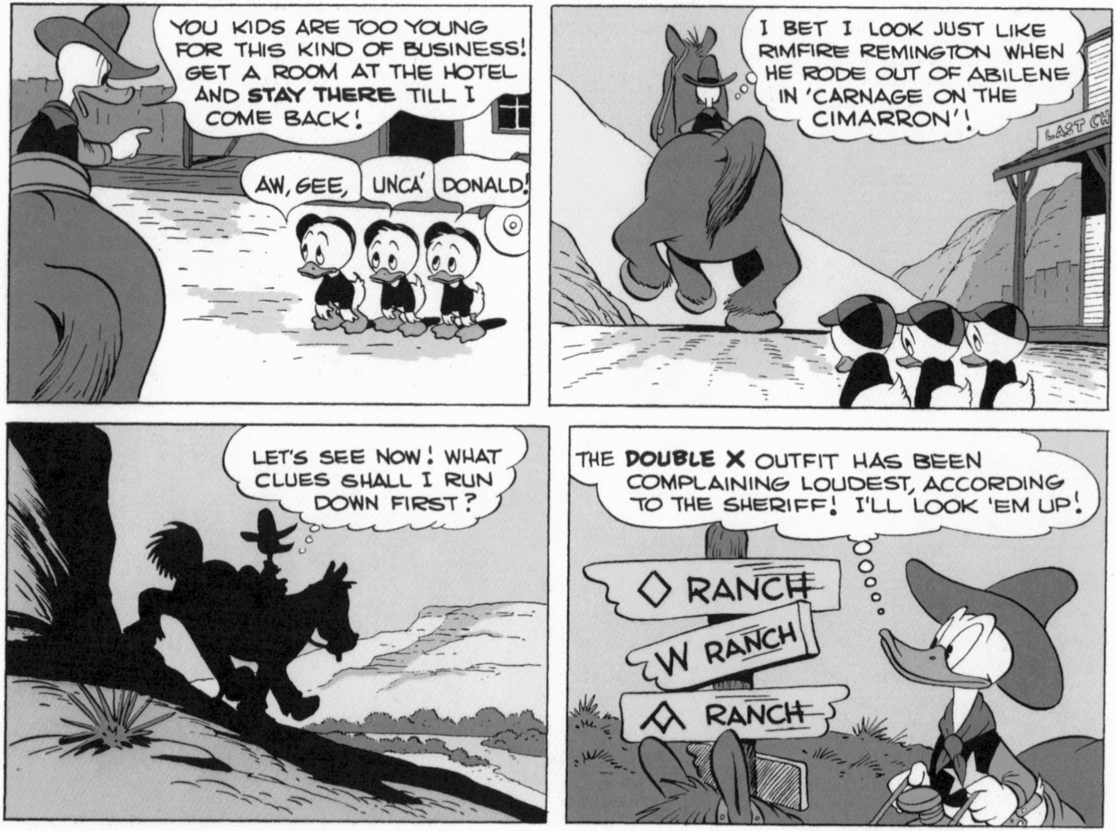
YOU KIDS ARE TOO YOUNG FOR THIS KIND OF BUSINESS! GET A ROOM AT THE HOTEL AND **STAY THERE** TILL I COME BACK!
AW, GEE,
UNCA'
DONALD!
I BET I LOOK JUST LIKE RIMFIRE REMINGTON WHEN HE RODE OUT OF ABILENE IN 'CARNAGE ON THE CIMARRON'!
LET'S SEE NOW! WHAT CLUES SHALL I RUN DOWN FIRST?
THE **DOUBLE X** OUTFIT HAS BEEN COMPLAINING LOUDEST, ACCORDING TO THE SHERIFF! I'LL LOOK 'EM UP!
RANCH
W RANCH
RANCH

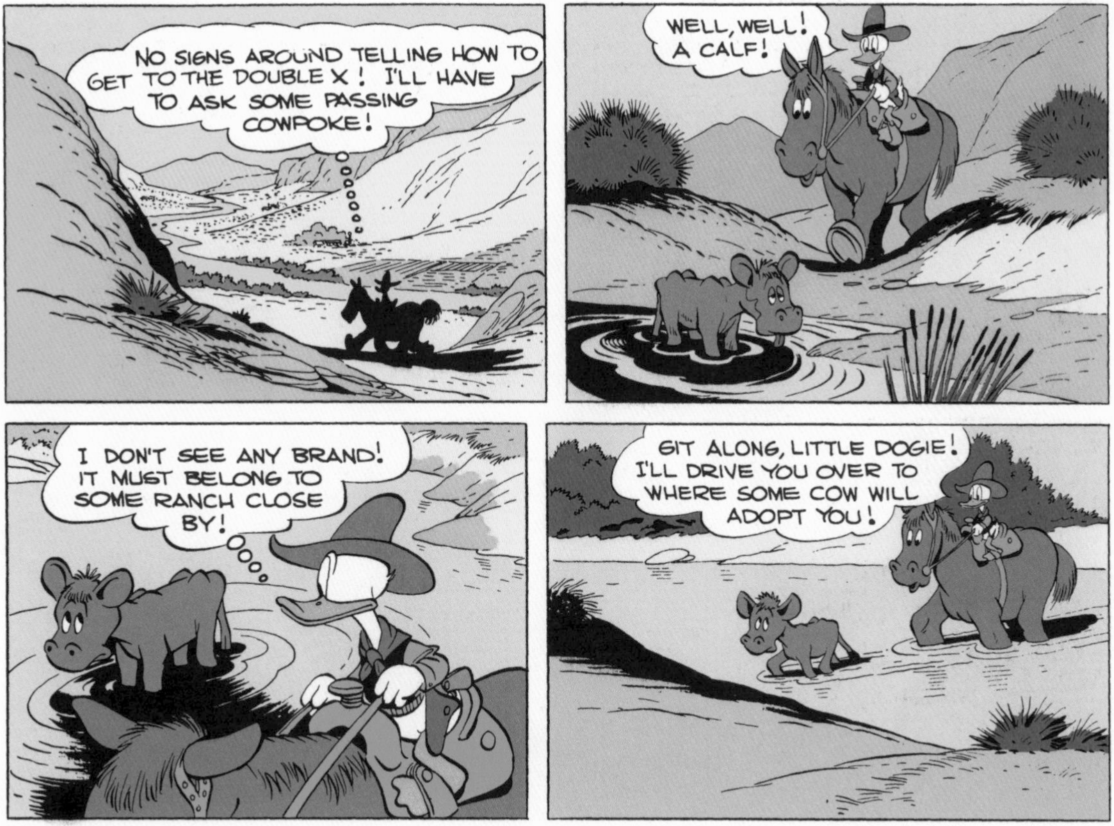
NO SIGNS AROUND TELLING HOW TO GET TO THE DOUBLE X! I'LL HAVE TO ASK SOME PASSING COWPOKE!
WELL, WELL! A CALF!
I DON'T SEE ANY BRAND! IT MUST BELONG TO SOME RANCH CLOSE BY!
GIT ALONG, LITTLE DOGIE! I'LL DRIVE YOU OVER TO WHERE SOME COW WILL ADOPT YOU!

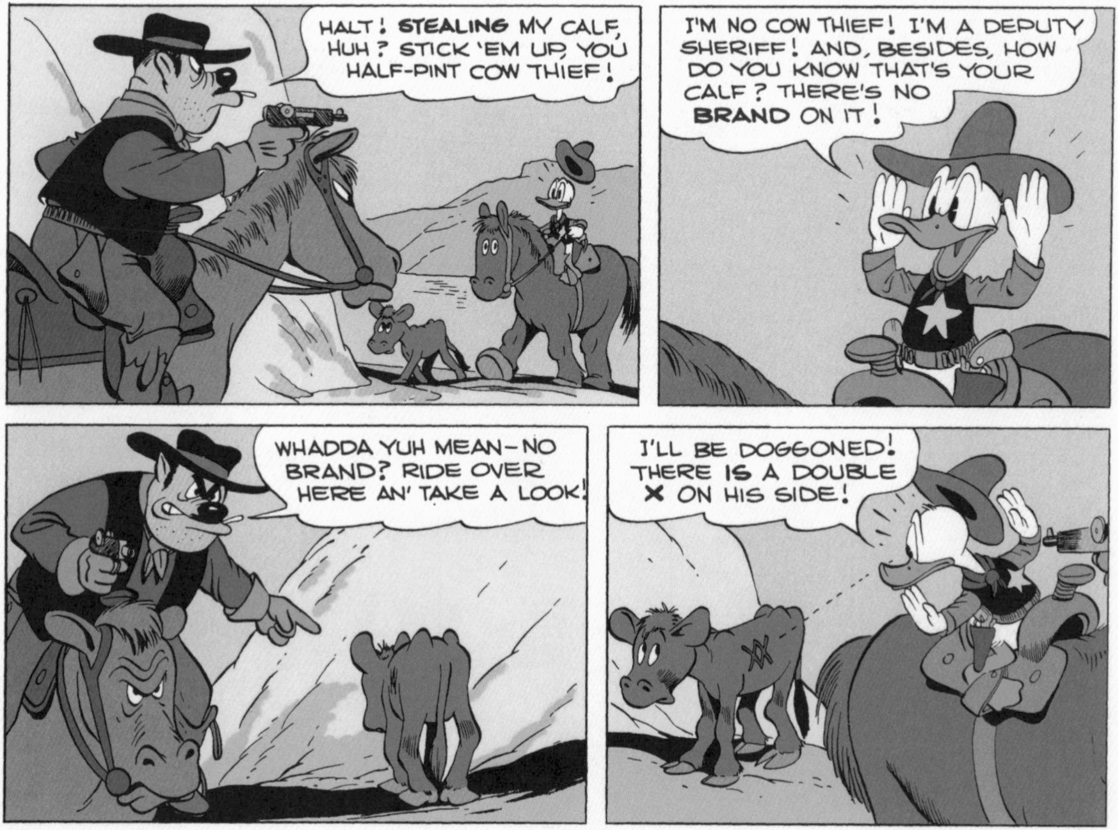
HALT! STEALING MY CALF, HUH? STICK 'EM UP, YOU HALF-PINT COW THIEF!
I'M NO COW THIEF! I'M A DEPUTY SHERIFF! AND, BESIDES, HOW DO YOU KNOW THAT'S YOUR CALF? THERE'S NO BRAND ON IT!
WHADDA YUH MEAN—NO BRAND? RIDE OVER HERE AN' TAKE A LOOK!
I'LL BE DOGGONED! THERE IS A DOUBLE X ON HIS SIDE!

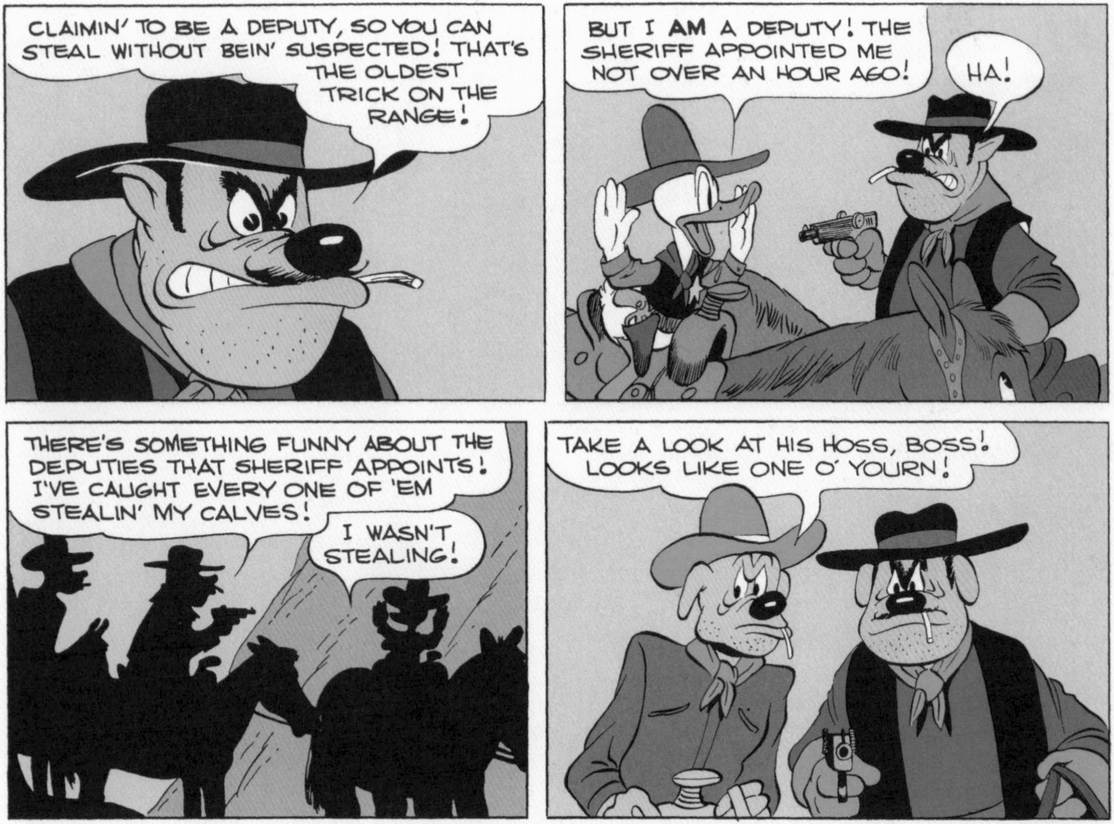
CLAIMIN' TO BE A DEPUTY, SO YOU CAN STEAL WITHOUT BEIN' SUSPECTED! THAT'S THE OLDEST TRICK ON THE RANGE!
BUT I **AM** A DEPUTY! THE SHERIFF APPOINTED ME NOT OVER AN HOUR AGO!
HA!
THERE'S SOMETHING FUNNY ABOUT THE DEPUTIES THAT SHERIFF APPOINTS! I'VE CAUGHT EVERY ONE OF 'EM STEALIN' MY CALVES!
I WASN'T STEALING!
TAKE A LOOK AT HIS HOSS, BOSS! LOOKS LIKE ONE O' YOURN!

IT **IS** ONE OF MINE! THERE'S MY DOUBLE X BRAND! RIGHT IN PLAIN SIGHT!
AND **MY BRAND** ON THE SADDLE, TOO!
I DIDN'T SEE THOSE BRANDS UNTIL THIS MINUTE!
YOU TALK **TOO DUMB**! GET OFFA MY HORSE BEFORE I BLOW YOU OFF!

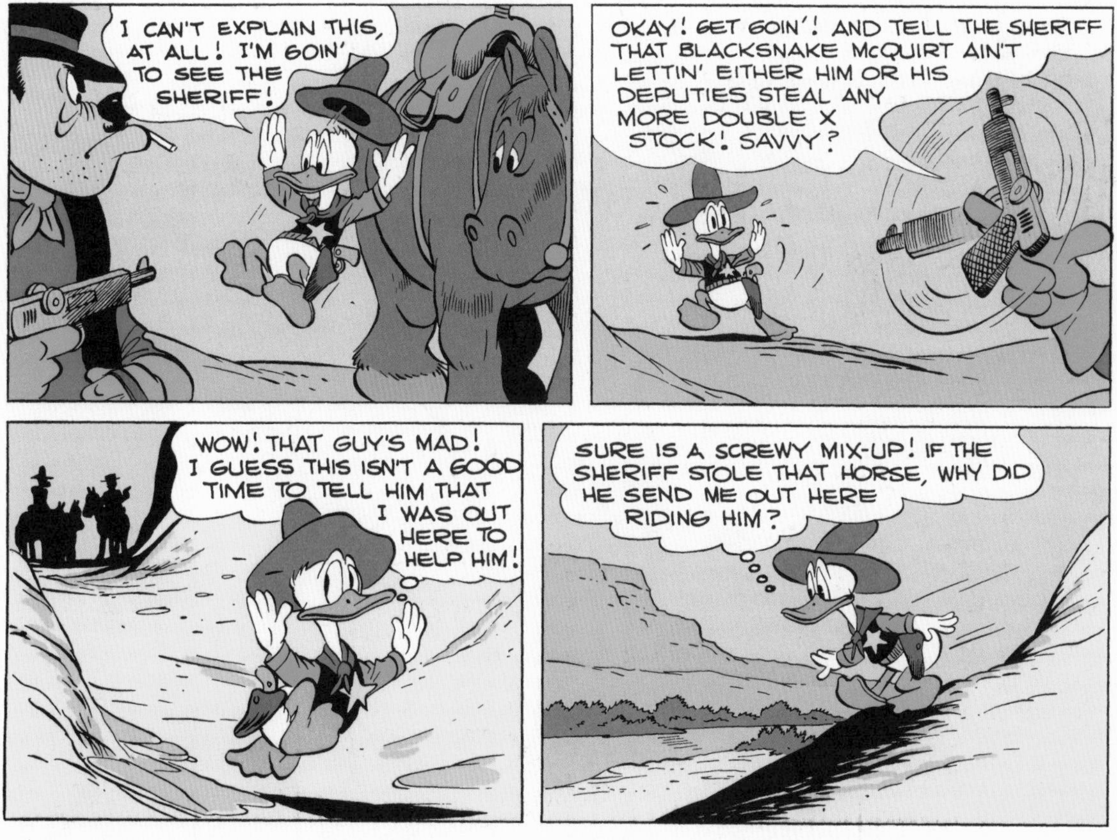
I CAN'T EXPLAIN THIS, AT ALL! I'M GOIN' TO SEE THE SHERIFF!
OKAY! GET GOIN'! AND TELL THE SHERIFF THAT BLACKSNAKE McQUIRT AIN'T LETTIN' EITHER HIM OR HIS DEPUTIES STEAL ANY MORE DOUBLE X STOCK! SAVVY?
WOW! THAT GUY'S MAD! I GUESS THIS ISN'T A GOOD TIME TO TELL HIM THAT I WAS OUT HERE TO HELP HIM!
SURE IS A SCREWY MIX-UP! IF THE SHERIFF STOLE THAT HORSE, WHY DID HE SEND ME OUT HERE RIDING HIM?

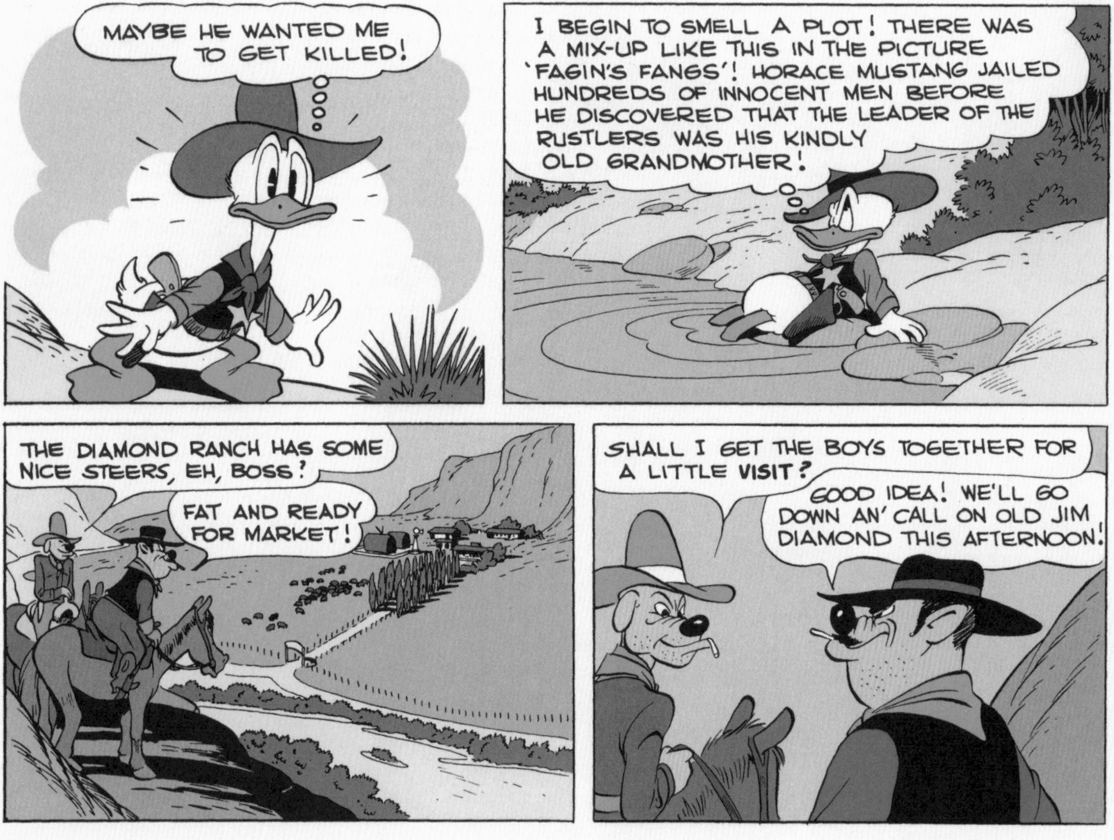
MAYBE HE WANTED ME TO GET KILLED!
I BEGIN TO SMELL A PLOT! THERE WAS A MIX-UP LIKE THIS IN THE PICTURE 'FAGIN'S FANGS'! HORACE MUSTANG JAILED HUNDREDS OF INNOCENT MEN BEFORE HE DISCOVERED THAT THE LEADER OF THE RUSTLERS WAS HIS KINDLY OLD GRANDMOTHER!
THE DIAMOND RANCH HAS SOME NICE STEERS, EH, BOSS?
FAT AND READY FOR MARKET!
SHALL I GET THE BOYS TOGETHER FOR A LITTLE **VISIT**?
GOOD IDEA! WE'LL GO DOWN AN' CALL ON OLD JIM DIAMOND THIS AFTERNOON!

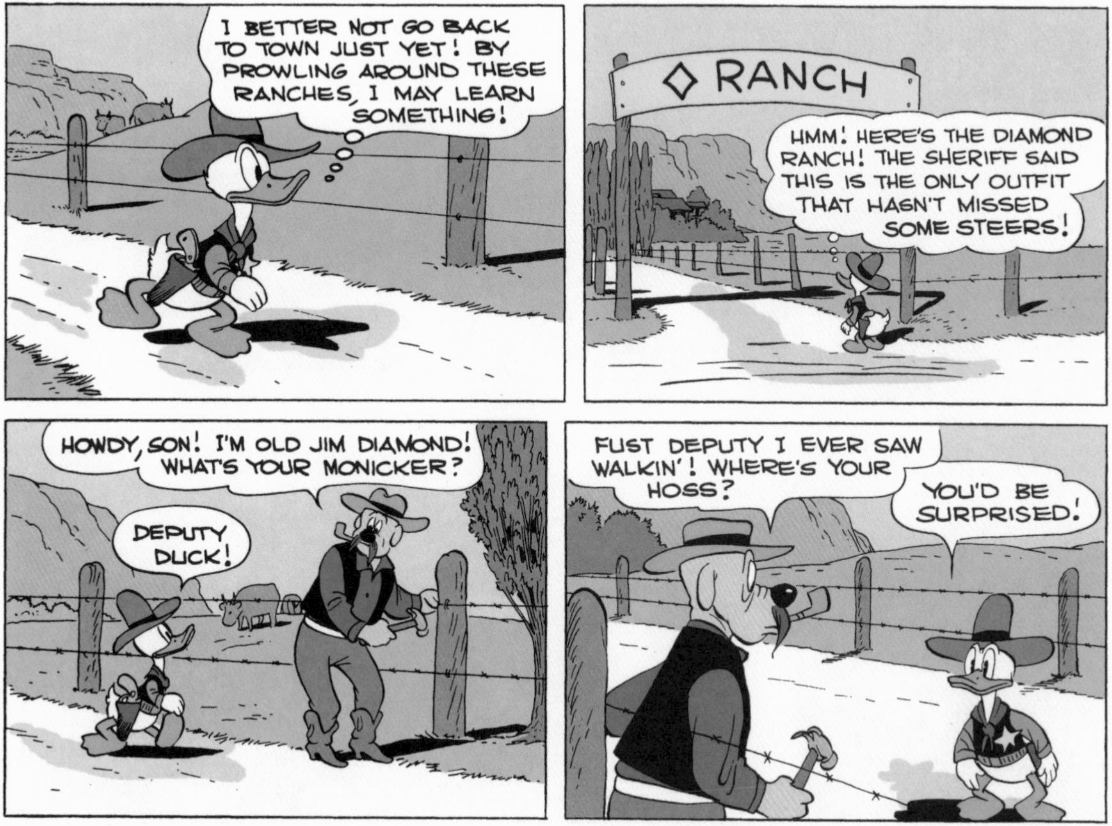
I BETTER NOT GO BACK TO TOWN JUST YET! BY PROWLING AROUND THESE RANCHES, I MAY LEARN SOMETHING!
◇ RANCH
HMM! HERE'S THE DIAMOND RANCH! THE SHERIFF SAID THIS IS THE ONLY OUTFIT THAT HASN'T MISSED SOME STEERS!
HOWDY, SON! I'M OLD JIM DIAMOND! WHAT'S YOUR MONICKER?
DEPUTY DUCK!
FUST DEPUTY I EVER SAW WALKIN'! WHERE'S YOUR HOSS?
YOU'D BE SURPRISED!

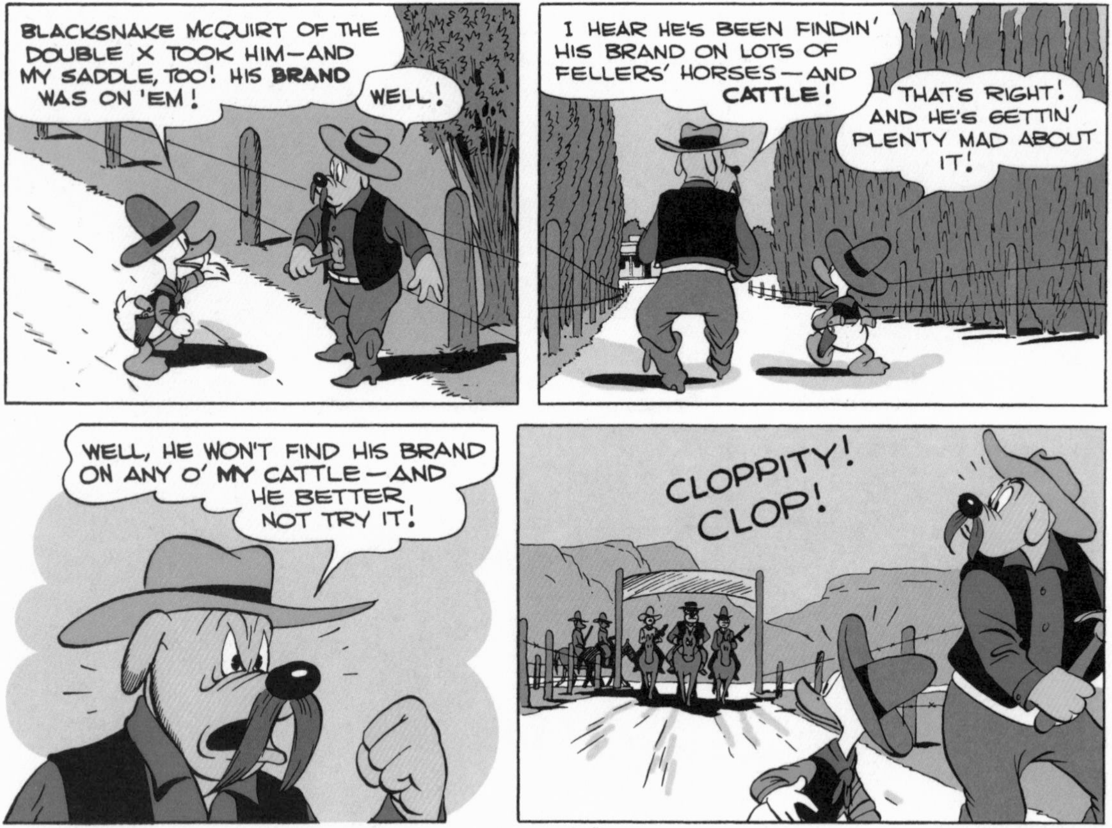
BLACKSNAKE McQUIRT OF THE DOUBLE X TOOK HIM—AND MY SADDLE, TOO! HIS BRAND WAS ON 'EM!
WELL!
I HEAR HE'S BEEN FINDIN' HIS BRAND ON LOTS OF FELLERS' HORSES—AND CATTLE!
THAT'S RIGHT! AND HE'S GETTIN' PLENTY MAD ABOUT IT!
WELL, HE WON'T FIND HIS BRAND ON ANY O' MY CATTLE—AND HE BETTER NOT TRY IT!
CLOPPITY! CLOP!

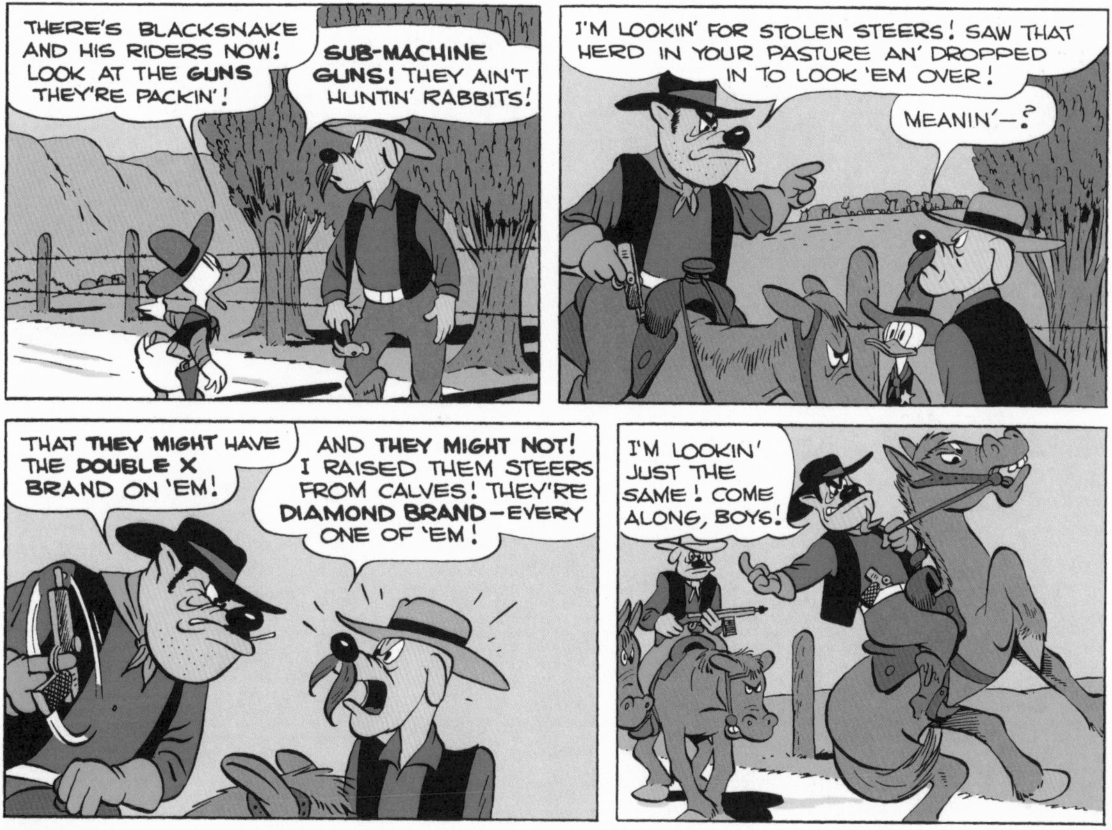
THERE'S BLACKSNAKE AND HIS RIDERS NOW! LOOK AT THE **GUNS** THEY'RE PACKIN'!
SUB-MACHINE GUNS! THEY AIN'T HUNTIN' RABBITS!
I'M LOOKIN' FOR STOLEN STEERS! SAW THAT HERD IN YOUR PASTURE AN' DROPPED IN TO LOOK 'EM OVER!
MEANIN'—?
THAT **THEY MIGHT** HAVE THE **DOUBLE X** BRAND ON 'EM!
AND **THEY MIGHT NOT!** I RAISED THEM STEERS FROM CALVES! THEY'RE **DIAMOND BRAND**—EVERY ONE OF 'EM!
I'M LOOKIN' JUST THE SAME! COME ALONG, BOYS!

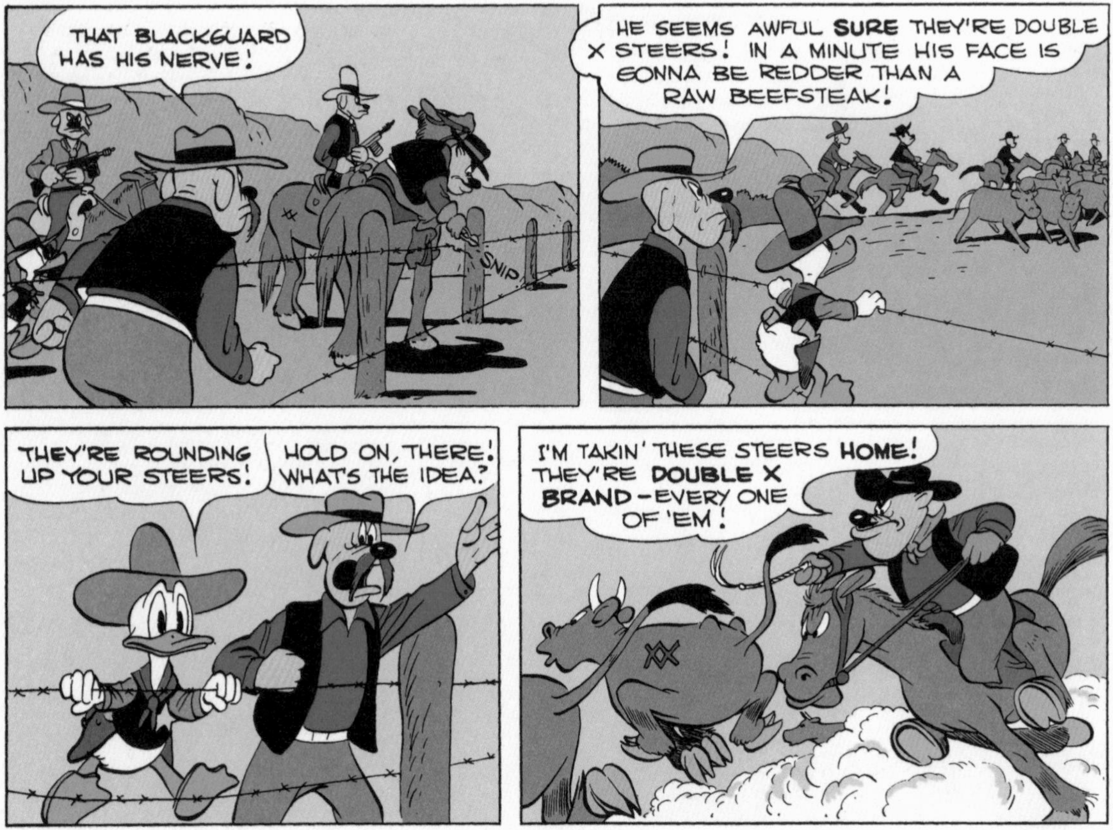
THAT BLACKGUARD HAS HIS NERVE!
SNIP
HE SEEMS AWFUL **SURE** THEY'RE DOUBLE X STEERS! IN A MINUTE HIS FACE IS GONNA BE REDDER THAN A RAW BEEFSTEAK!
THEY'RE ROUNDING UP YOUR STEERS!
HOLD ON, THERE! WHAT'S THE IDEA?
I'M TAKIN' THESE STEERS **HOME!** THEY'RE **DOUBLE X BRAND**—EVERY ONE OF 'EM!

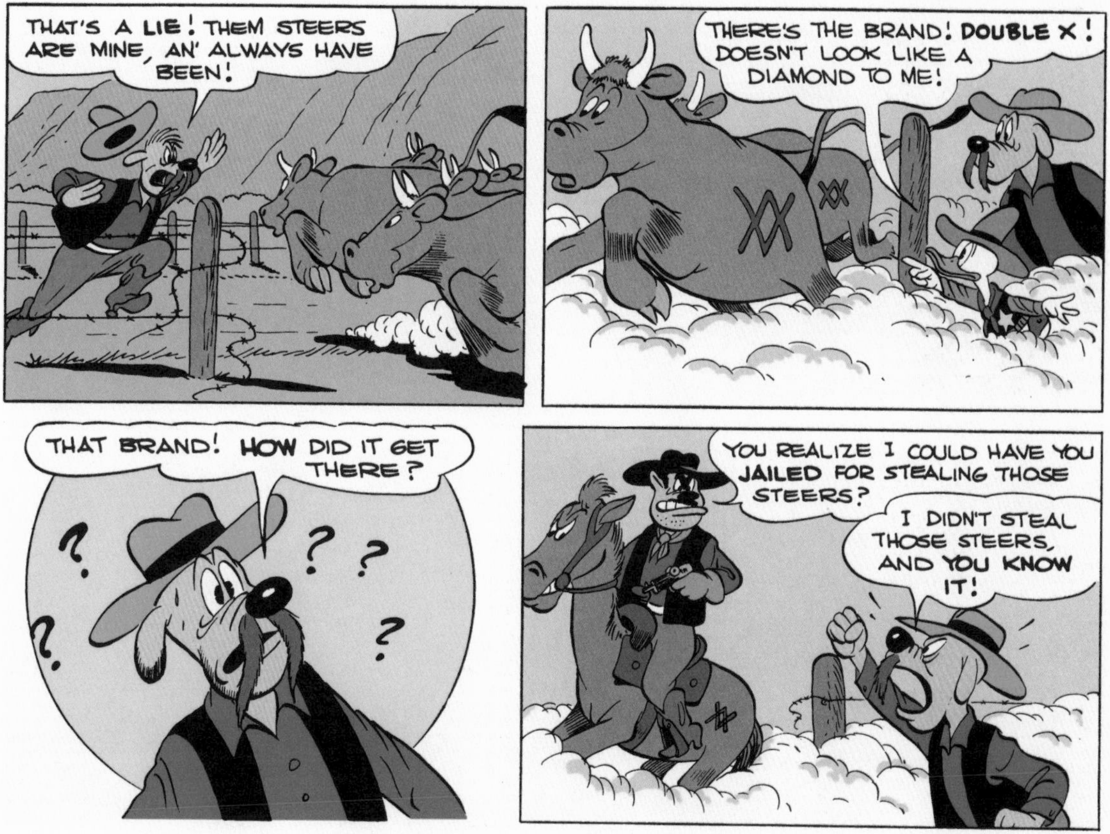
THAT'S A LIE! THEM STEERS ARE MINE, AN' ALWAYS HAVE BEEN!
THERE'S THE BRAND! DOUBLE X! DOESN'T LOOK LIKE A DIAMOND TO ME!
THAT BRAND! HOW DID IT GET THERE?
YOU REALIZE I COULD HAVE YOU JAILED FOR STEALING THOSE STEERS?
I DIDN'T STEAL THOSE STEERS, AND YOU KNOW IT!

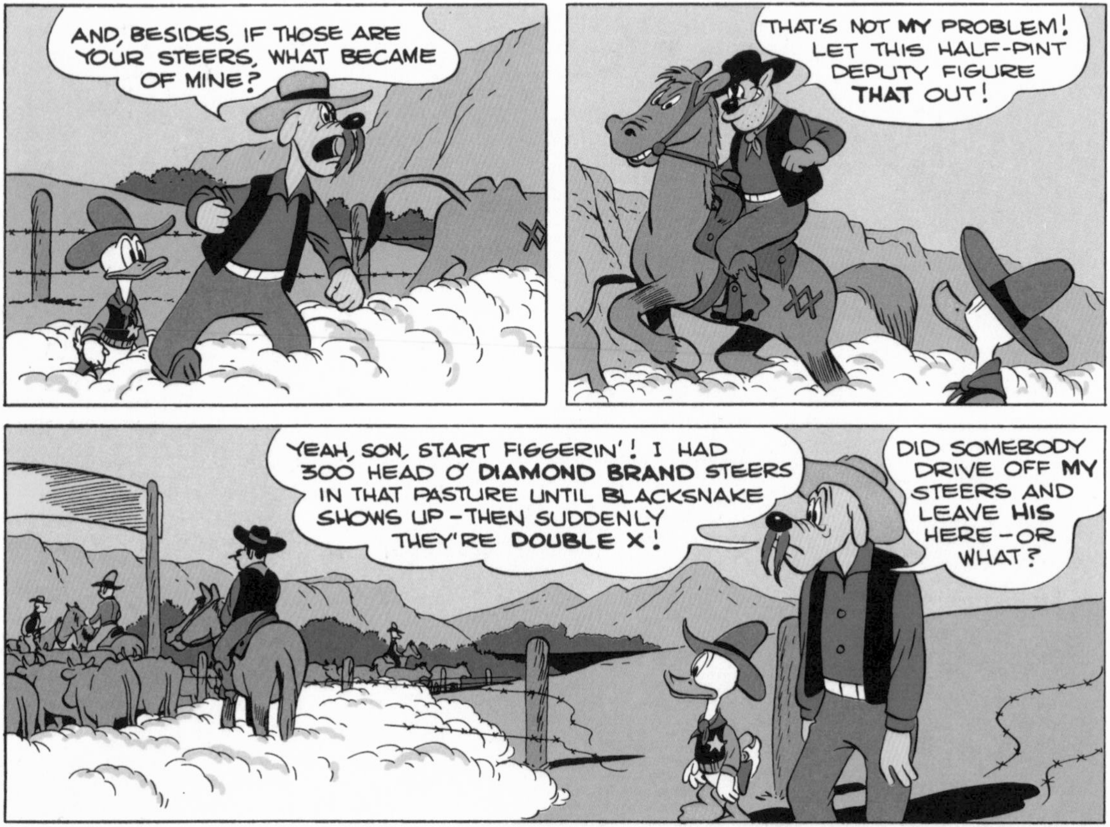
AND, BESIDES, IF THOSE ARE YOUR STEERS, WHAT BECAME OF MINE?
THAT'S NOT **MY** PROBLEM! LET THIS HALF-PINT DEPUTY FIGURE **THAT** OUT!
YEAH, SON, START FIGGERIN'! I HAD 300 HEAD O' **DIAMOND BRAND** STEERS IN THAT PASTURE UNTIL BLACKSNAKE SHOWS UP—THEN SUDDENLY THEY'RE **DOUBLE X**!
DID SOMEBODY DRIVE OFF **MY** STEERS AND LEAVE **HIS** HERE—OR WHAT?

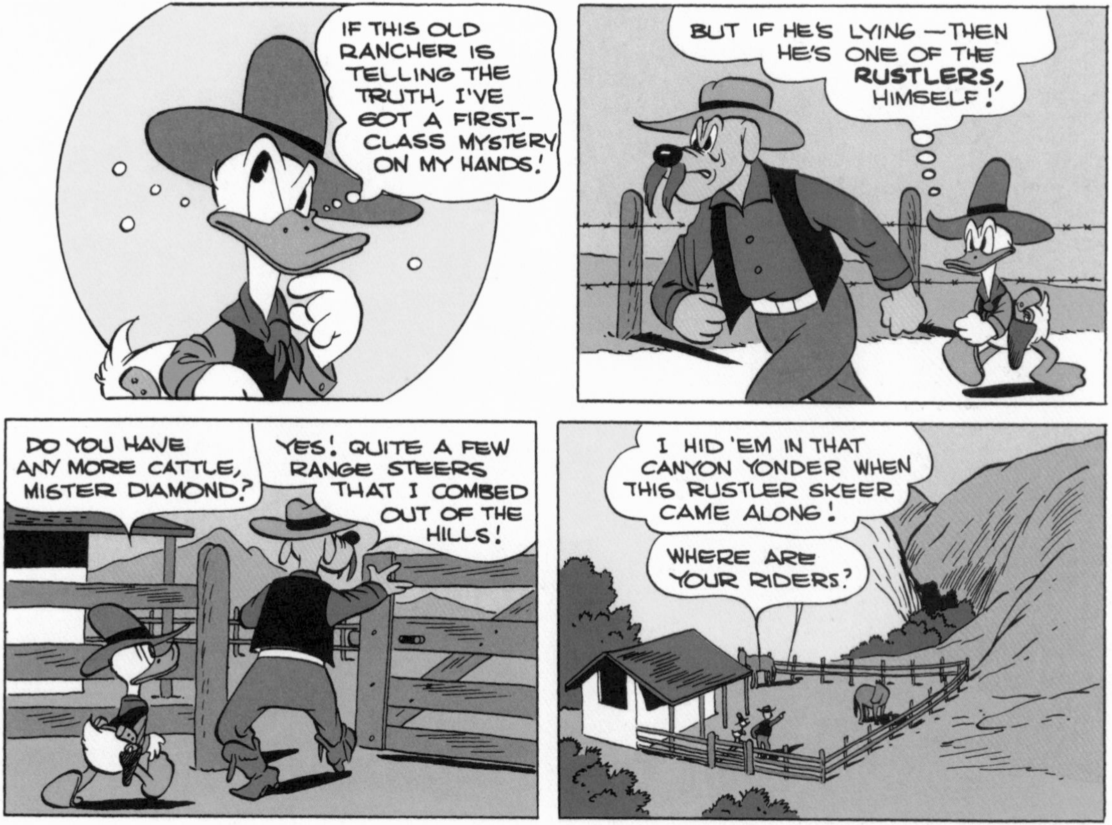
IF THIS OLD RANCHER IS TELLING THE TRUTH, I'VE GOT A FIRST-CLASS MYSTERY ON MY HANDS!
BUT IF HE'S LYING —THEN HE'S ONE OF THE **RUSTLERS**, HIMSELF!
DO YOU HAVE ANY MORE CATTLE, MISTER DIAMOND?
YES! QUITE A FEW RANGE STEERS THAT I COMBED OUT OF THE HILLS!
I HID 'EM IN THAT CANYON YONDER WHEN THIS RUSTLER SKEER CAME ALONG!
WHERE ARE YOUR RIDERS?

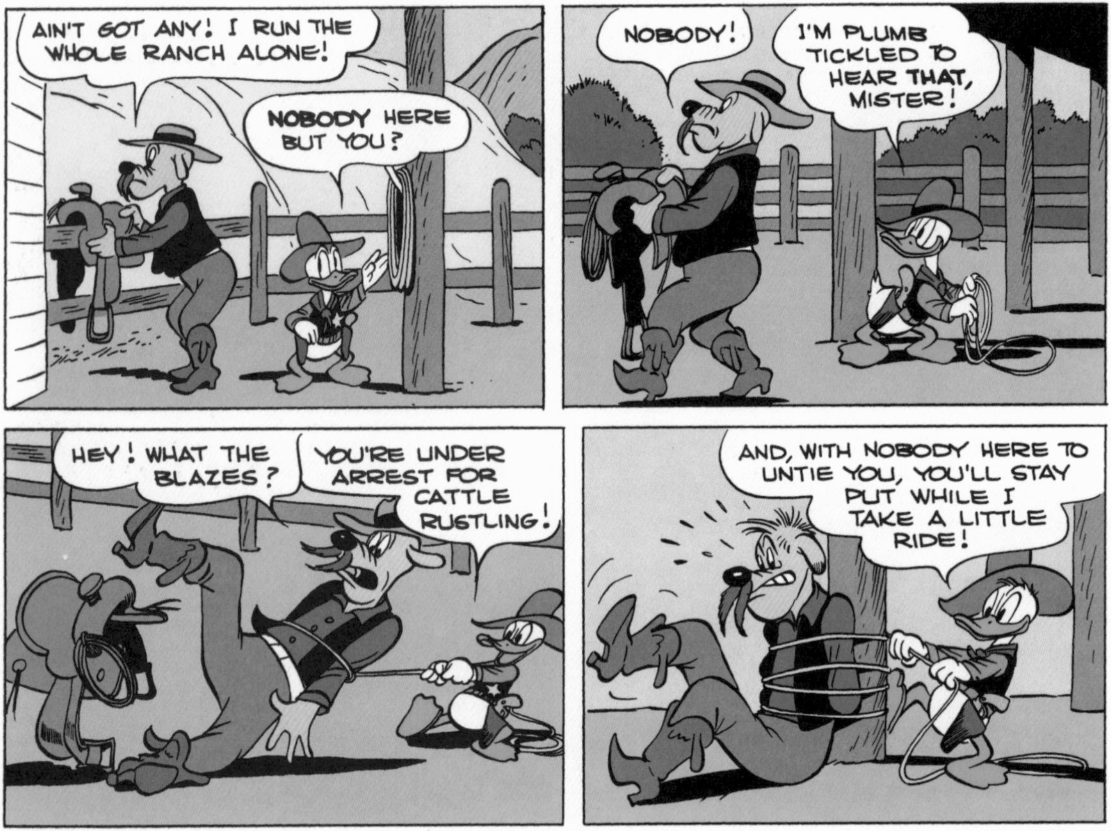
AIN'T GOT ANY! I RUN THE WHOLE RANCH ALONE!
NOBODY HERE BUT YOU?
NOBODY!
I'M PLUMB TICKLED TO HEAR THAT, MISTER!
HEY! WHAT THE BLAZES?
YOU'RE UNDER ARREST FOR CATTLE RUSTLING!
AND, WITH NOBODY HERE TO UNTIE YOU, YOU'LL STAY PUT WHILE I TAKE A LITTLE RIDE!

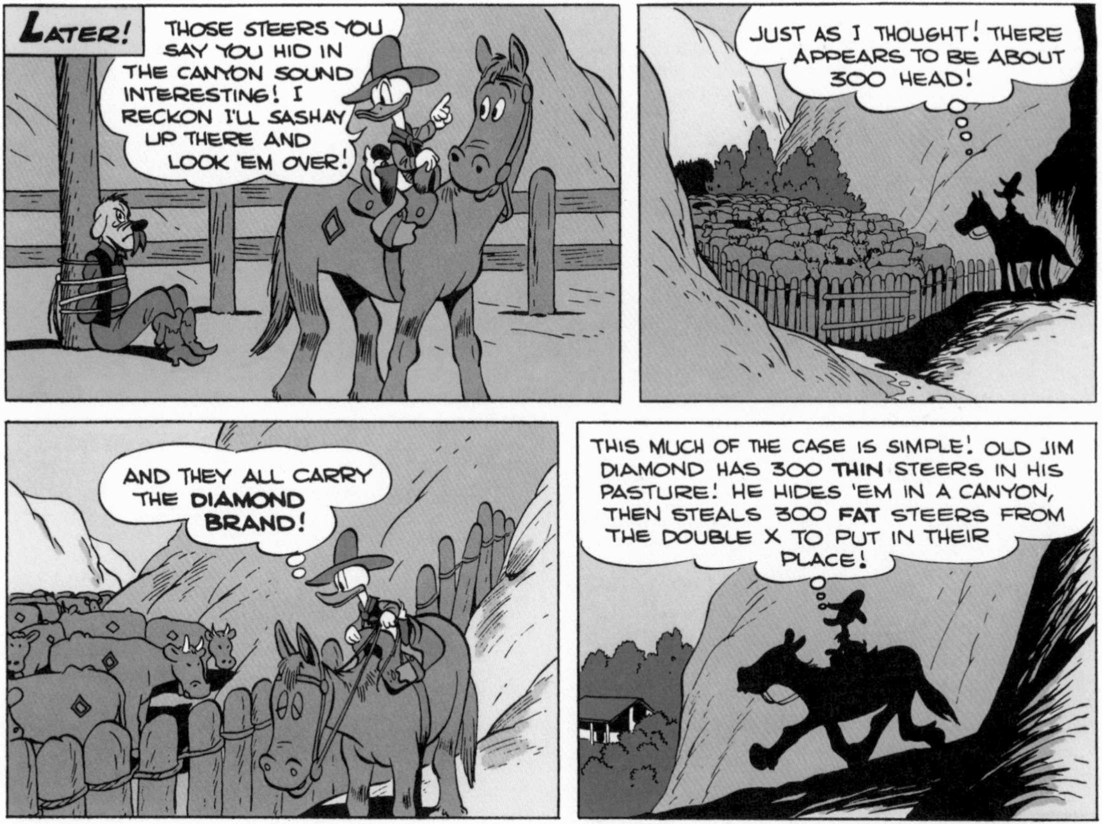
LATER!
THOSE STEERS YOU SAY YOU HID IN THE CANYON SOUND INTERESTING! I RECKON I'LL SASHAY UP THERE AND LOOK 'EM OVER!
JUST AS I THOUGHT! THERE APPEARS TO BE ABOUT 300 HEAD!
AND THEY ALL CARRY THE **DIAMOND BRAND**!
THIS MUCH OF THE CASE IS SIMPLE! OLD JIM DIAMOND HAS 300 **THIN** STEERS IN HIS PASTURE! HE HIDES 'EM IN A CANYON, THEN STEALS 300 **FAT** STEERS FROM THE DOUBLE X TO PUT IN THEIR PLACE!

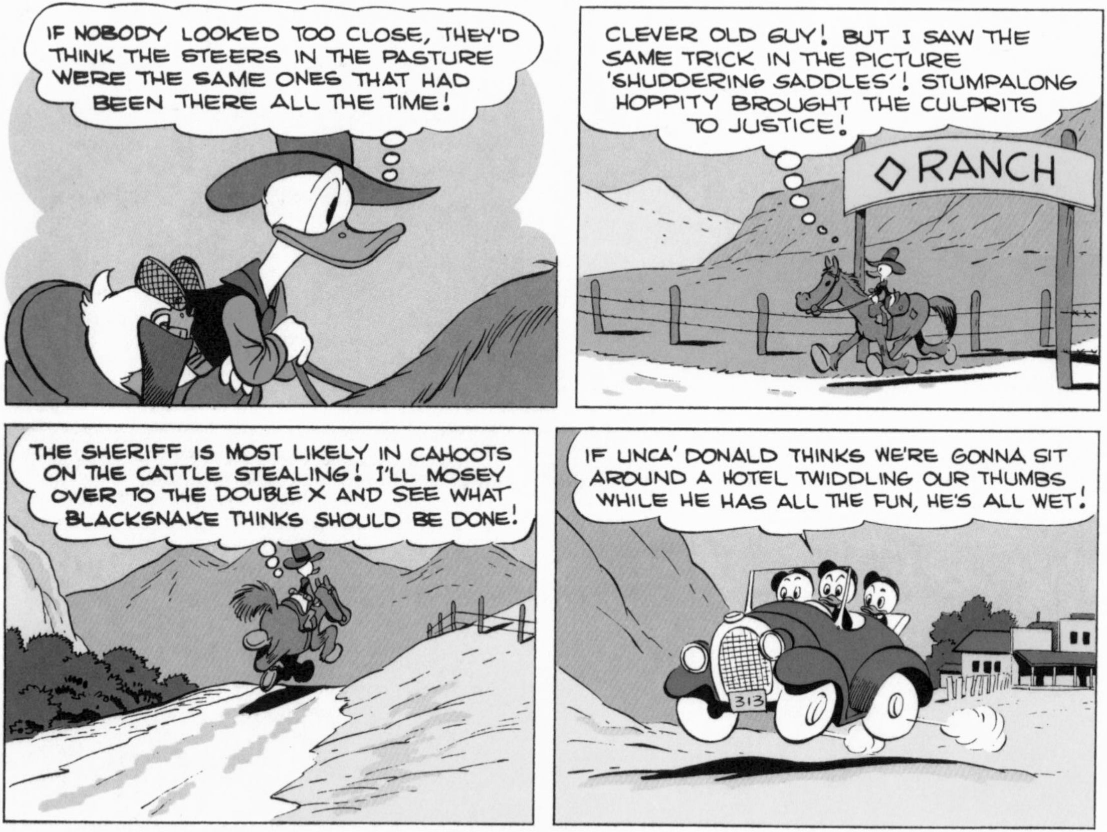
IF NOBODY LOOKED TOO CLOSE, THEY'D THINK THE STEERS IN THE PASTURE WERE THE SAME ONES THAT HAD BEEN THERE ALL THE TIME!
CLEVER OLD GUY! BUT I SAW THE SAME TRICK IN THE PICTURE 'SHUDDERING SADDLES'! STUMPALONG HOPPITY BROUGHT THE CULPRITS TO JUSTICE!
◇ RANCH
THE SHERIFF IS MOST LIKELY IN CAHOOTS ON THE CATTLE STEALING! I'LL MOSEY OVER TO THE DOUBLE X AND SEE WHAT BLACKSNAKE THINKS SHOULD BE DONE!
IF UNCA' DONALD THINKS WE'RE GONNA SIT AROUND A HOTEL TWIDDLING OUR THUMBS WHILE HE HAS ALL THE FUN, HE'S ALL WET!
313

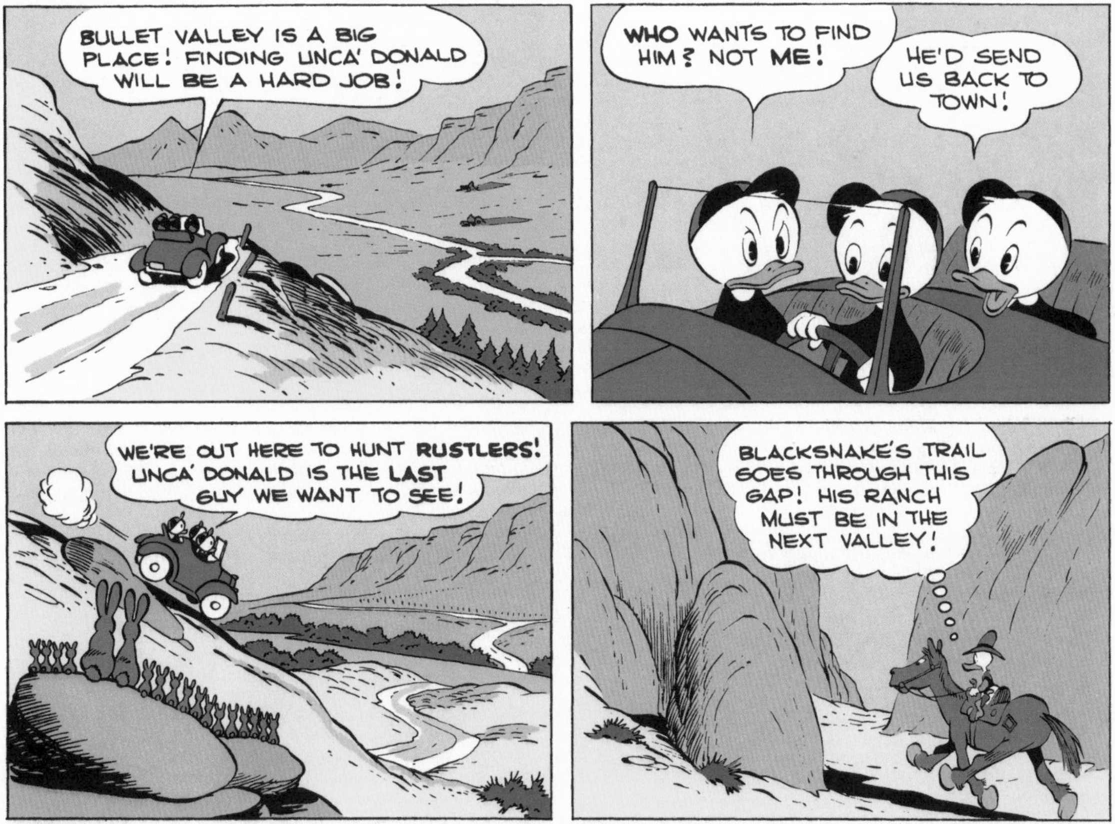
BULLET VALLEY IS A BIG PLACE! FINDING UNCA' DONALD WILL BE A HARD JOB!
WHO WANTS TO FIND HIM? NOT ME!
HE'D SEND US BACK TO TOWN!
WE'RE OUT HERE TO HUNT RUSTLERS! UNCA' DONALD IS THE LAST GUY WE WANT TO SEE!
BLACKSNAKE'S TRAIL GOES THROUGH THIS GAP! HIS RANCH MUST BE IN THE NEXT VALLEY!

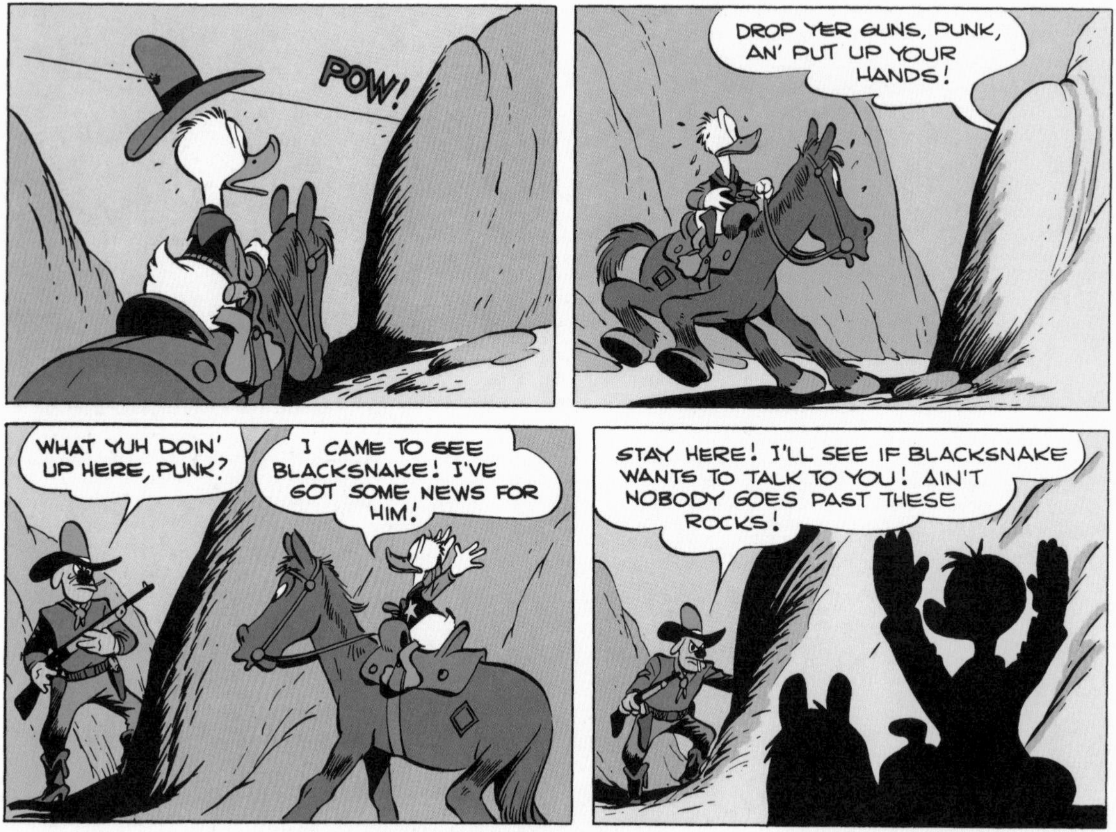
POW!
DROP YER GUNS, PUNK, AN' PUT UP YOUR HANDS!
WHAT YUH DOIN' UP HERE, PUNK?
I CAME TO SEE BLACKSNAKE! I'VE GOT SOME NEWS FOR HIM!
STAY HERE! I'LL SEE IF BLACKSNAKE WANTS TO TALK TO YOU! AIN'T NOBODY GOES PAST THESE ROCKS!

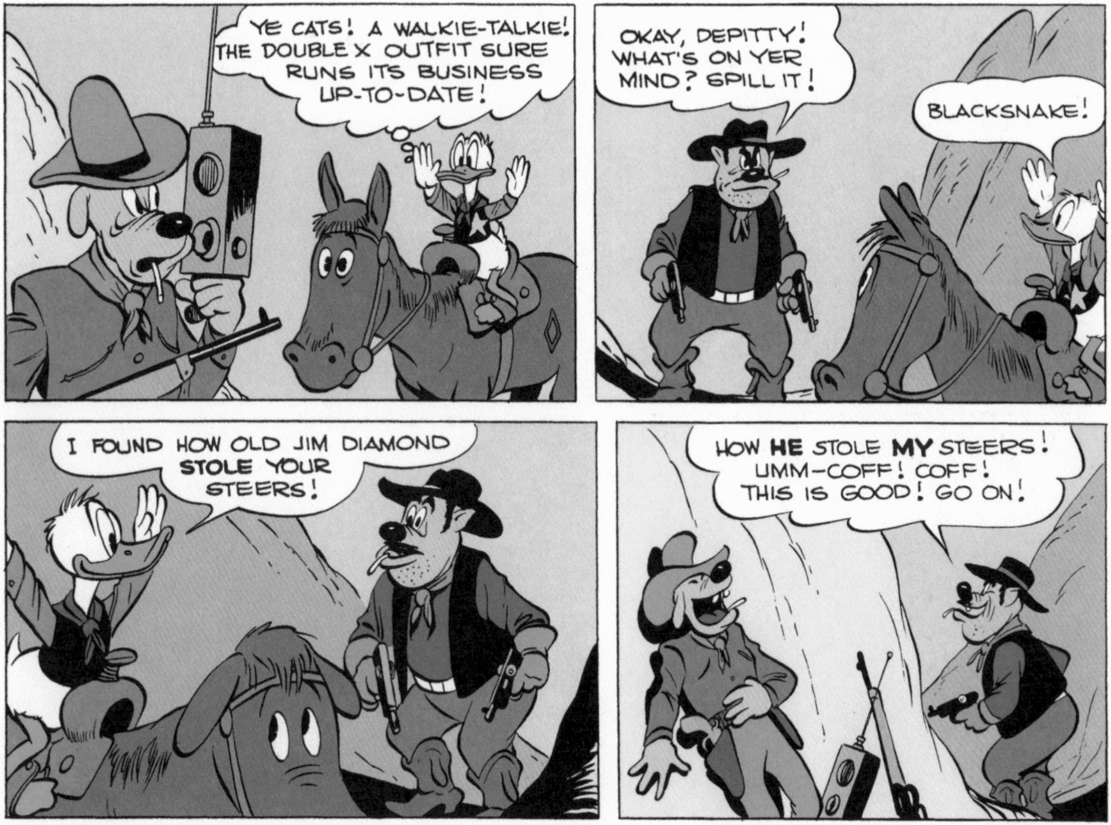
YE CATS! A WALKIE-TALKIE! THE DOUBLE X OUTFIT SURE RUNS ITS BUSINESS UP-TO-DATE!
OKAY, DEPITTY! WHAT'S ON YER MIND? SPILL IT!
BLACKSNAKE!
I FOUND HOW OLD JIM DIAMOND **STOLE** YOUR STEERS!
HOW **HE** STOLE **MY** STEERS! UMM-COFF! COFF! THIS IS GOOD! GO ON!

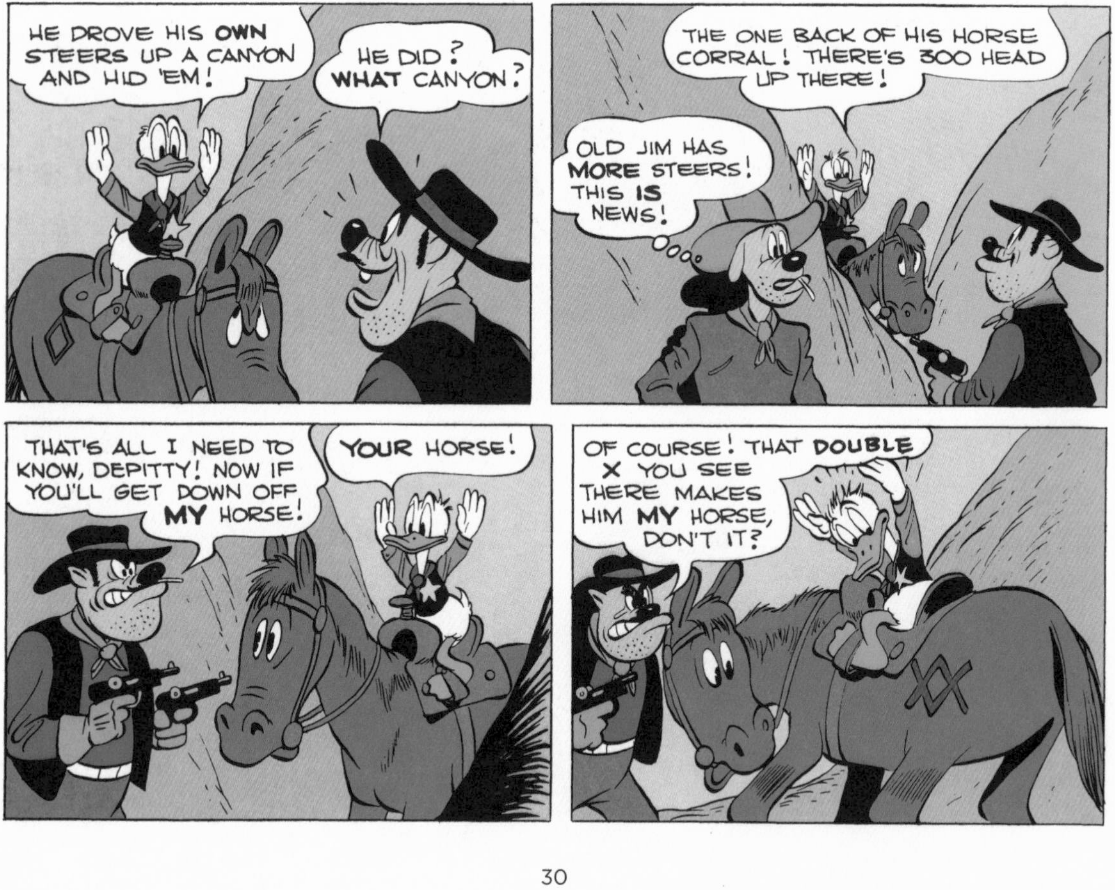
HE DROVE HIS **OWN** STEERS UP A CANYON AND HID 'EM!
HE DID? **WHAT** CANYON?
THE ONE BACK OF HIS HORSE CORRAL! THERE'S 300 HEAD UP THERE!
OLD JIM HAS **MORE** STEERS! THIS **IS** NEWS!
THAT'S ALL I NEED TO KNOW, DEPITTY! NOW IF YOU'LL GET DOWN OFF **MY** HORSE!
YOUR HORSE!
OF COURSE! THAT **DOUBLE X** YOU SEE THERE MAKES HIM **MY** HORSE, DON'T IT?

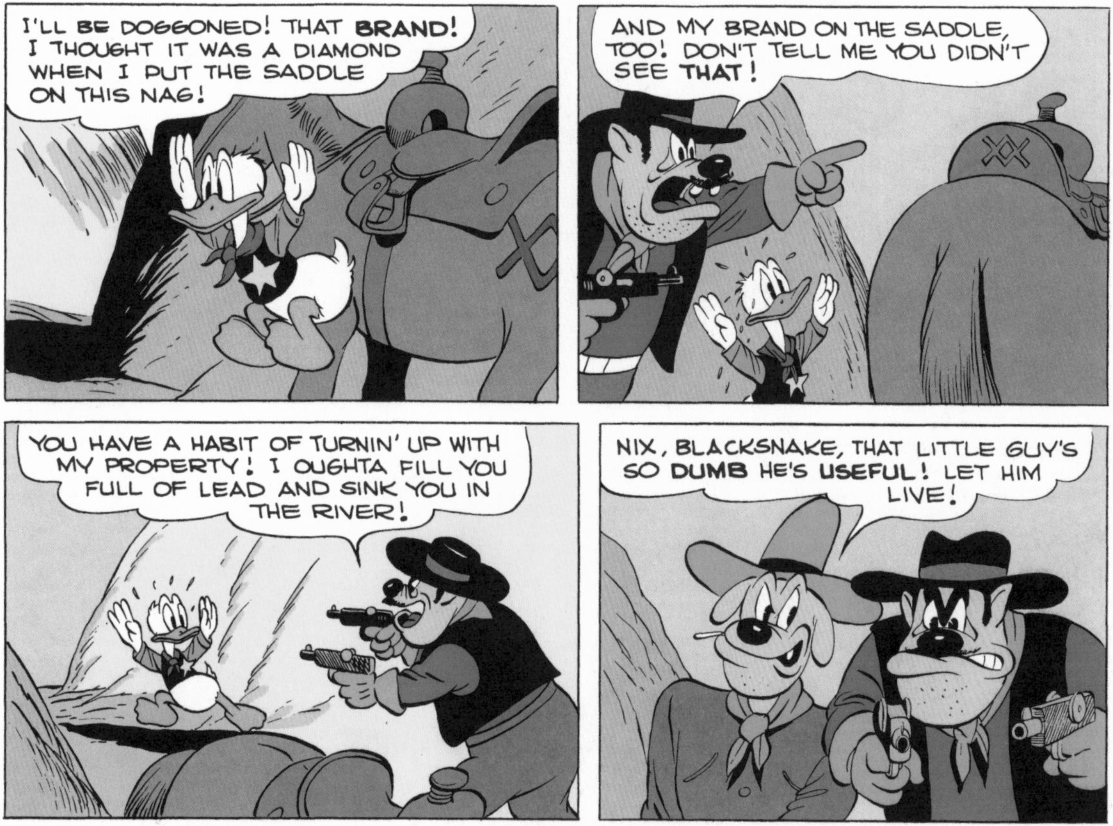
I'LL BE DOGGONED! THAT BRAND! I THOUGHT IT WAS A DIAMOND WHEN I PUT THE SADDLE ON THIS NAG!
AND MY BRAND ON THE SADDLE, TOO! DON'T TELL ME YOU DIDN'T SEE THAT!
YOU HAVE A HABIT OF TURNIN' UP WITH MY PROPERTY! I OUGHTA FILL YOU FULL OF LEAD AND SINK YOU IN THE RIVER!
NIX, BLACKSNAKE, THAT LITTLE GUY'S SO DUMB HE'S USEFUL! LET HIM LIVE!

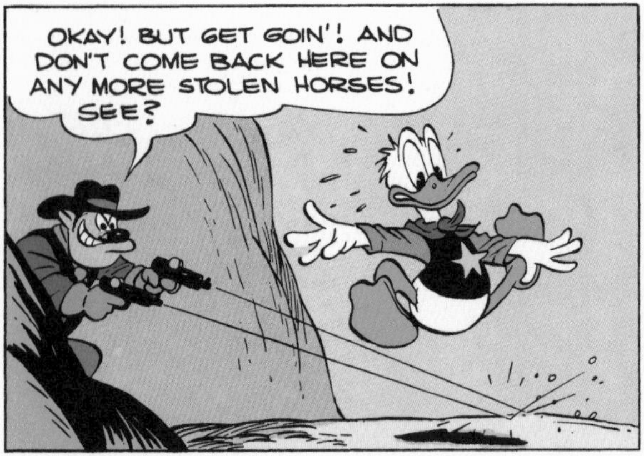
OKAY! BUT GET GOIN'! AND DON'T COME BACK HERE ON ANY MORE STOLEN HORSES! SEE?

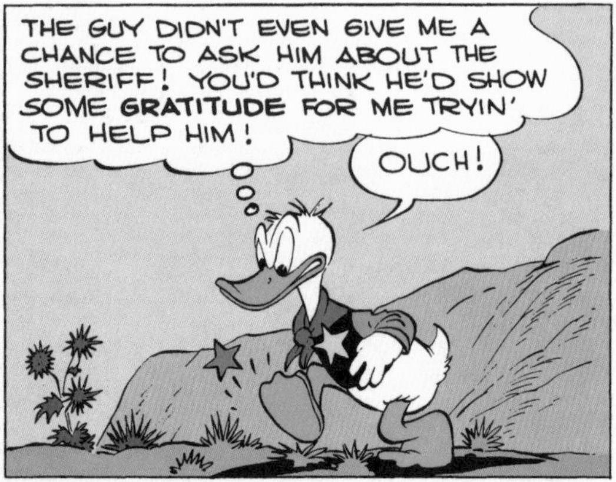
THE GUY DIDN'T EVEN GIVE ME A CHANCE TO ASK HIM ABOUT THE SHERIFF! YOU'D THINK HE'D SHOW SOME GRATITUDE FOR ME TRYIN' TO HELP HIM!
OUCH!

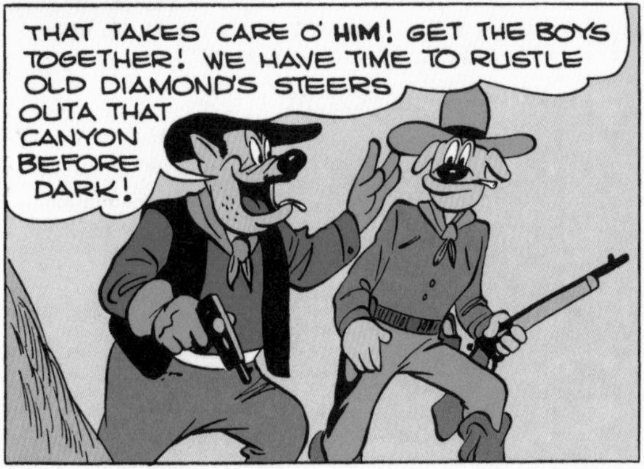
THAT TAKES CARE O' HIM! GET THE BOYS TOGETHER! WE HAVE TIME TO RUSTLE OLD DIAMOND'S STEERS OUTA THAT CANYON BEFORE DARK!

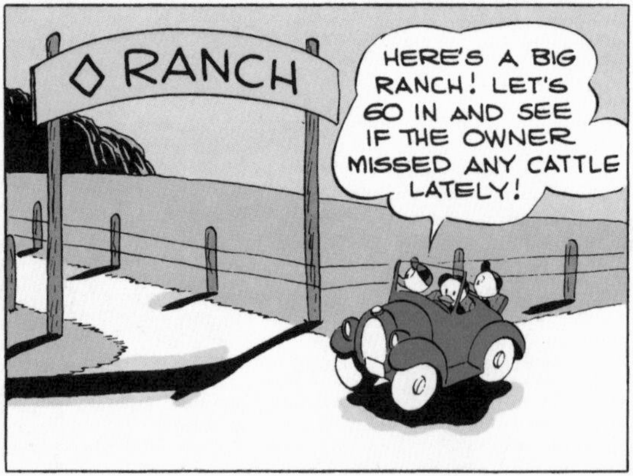
RANCH
HERE'S A BIG RANCH! LET'S GO IN AND SEE IF THE OWNER MISSED ANY CATTLE LATELY!

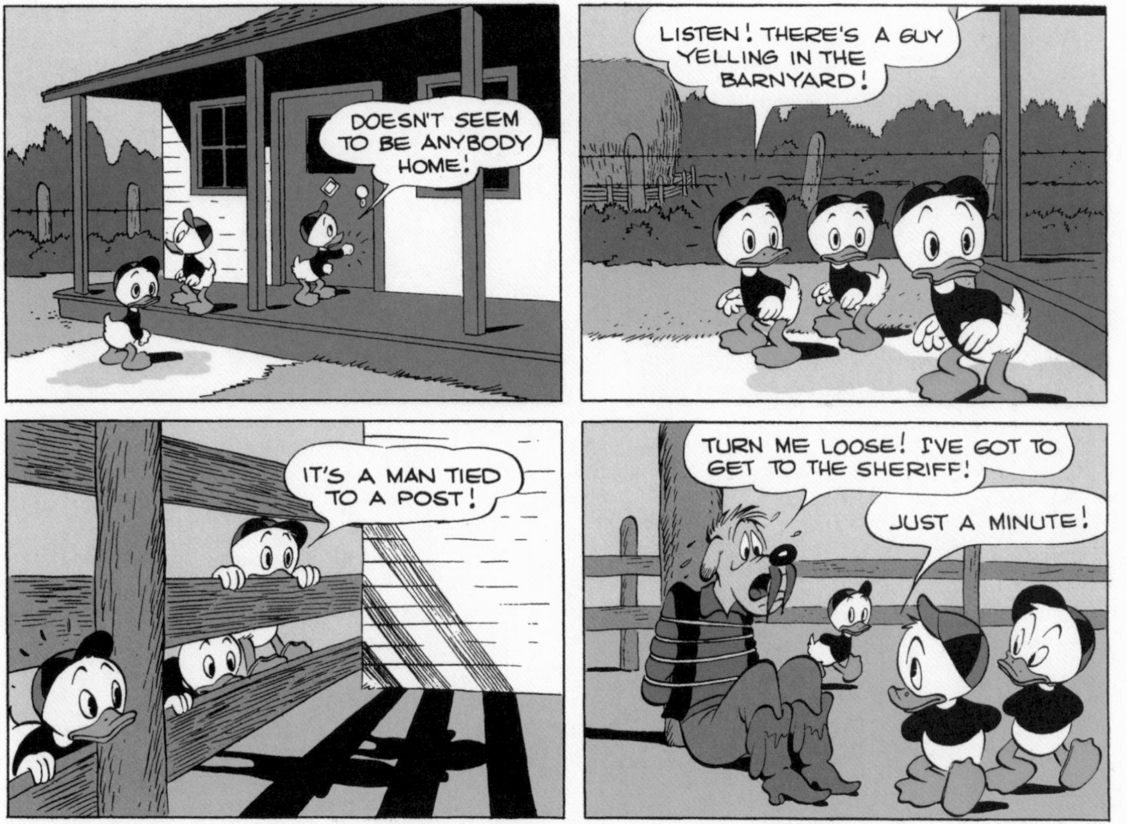
DOESN'T SEEM TO BE ANYBODY HOME!
LISTEN! THERE'S A GUY YELLING IN THE BARNYARD!
IT'S A MAN TIED TO A POST!
TURN ME LOOSE! I'VE GOT TO GET TO THE SHERIFF!
JUST A MINUTE!

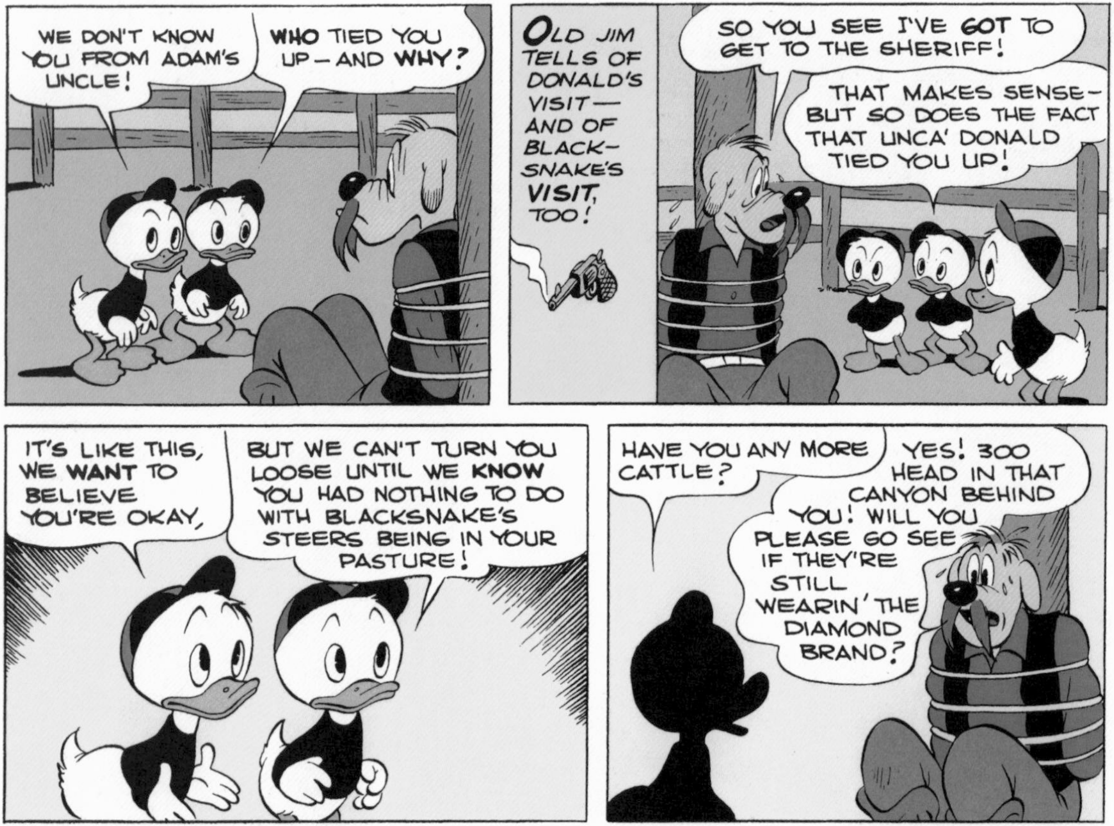
WE DON'T KNOW YOU FROM ADAM'S UNCLE!
WHO TIED YOU UP—AND WHY?
OLD JIM TELLS OF DONALD'S VISIT— AND OF BLACK-SNAKE'S VISIT, TOO!
SO YOU SEE I'VE GOT TO GET TO THE SHERIFF!
THAT MAKES SENSE— BUT SO DOES THE FACT THAT UNCA' DONALD TIED YOU UP!
IT'S LIKE THIS, WE WANT TO BELIEVE YOU'RE OKAY,
BUT WE CAN'T TURN YOU LOOSE UNTIL WE KNOW YOU HAD NOTHING TO DO WITH BLACKSNAKE'S STEERS BEING IN YOUR PASTURE!
HAVE YOU ANY MORE CATTLE?
YES! 300 HEAD IN THAT CANYON BEHIND YOU! WILL YOU PLEASE GO SEE IF THEY'RE STILL WEARIN' THE DIAMOND BRAND?

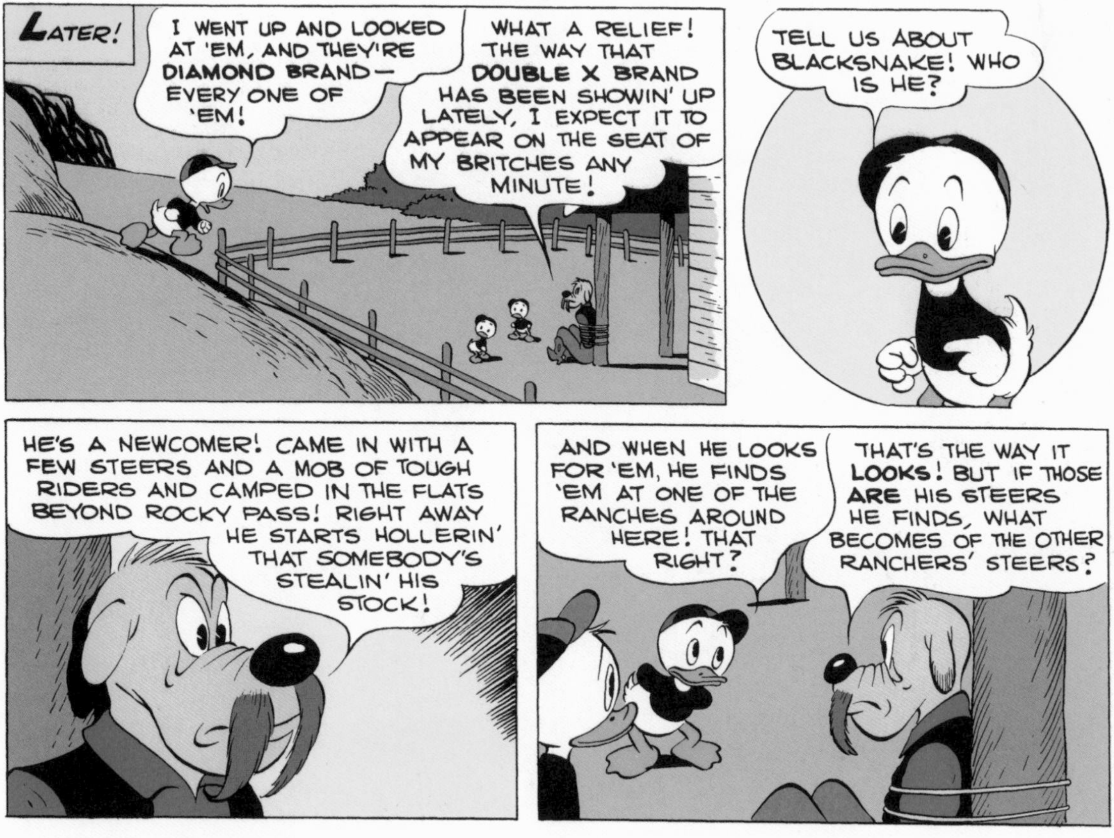
LATER!
I WENT UP AND LOOKED AT 'EM, AND THEY'RE **DIAMOND BRAND**— EVERY ONE OF 'EM!
WHAT A RELIEF! THE WAY THAT **DOUBLE X BRAND** HAS BEEN SHOWIN' UP LATELY, I EXPECT IT TO APPEAR ON THE SEAT OF MY BRITCHES ANY MINUTE!
TELL US ABOUT BLACKSNAKE! WHO IS HE?
HE'S A NEWCOMER! CAME IN WITH A FEW STEERS AND A MOB OF TOUGH RIDERS AND CAMPED IN THE FLATS BEYOND ROCKY PASS! RIGHT AWAY HE STARTS HOLLERIN' THAT SOMEBODY'S STEALIN' HIS STOCK!
AND WHEN HE LOOKS FOR 'EM, HE FINDS 'EM AT ONE OF THE RANCHES AROUND HERE! THAT RIGHT?
THAT'S THE WAY IT **LOOKS**! BUT IF THOSE **ARE** HIS STEERS HE FINDS, WHAT BECOMES OF THE OTHER RANCHERS' STEERS?

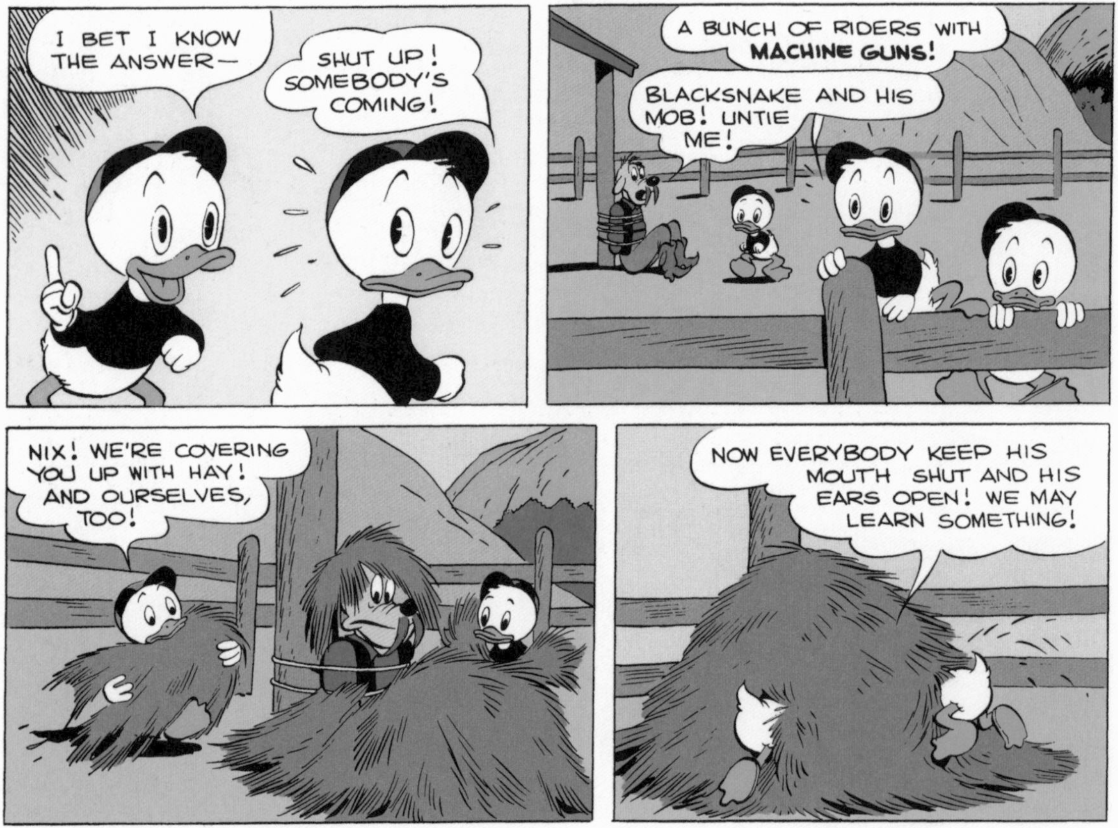
I BET I KNOW THE ANSWER—
SHUT UP! SOMEBODY'S COMING!
A BUNCH OF RIDERS WITH **MACHINE GUNS**!
BLACKSNAKE AND HIS MOB! UNTIE ME!
NIX! WE'RE COVERING YOU UP WITH HAY! AND OURSELVES, TOO!
NOW EVERYBODY KEEP HIS MOUTH SHUT AND HIS EARS OPEN! WE MAY LEARN SOMETHING!

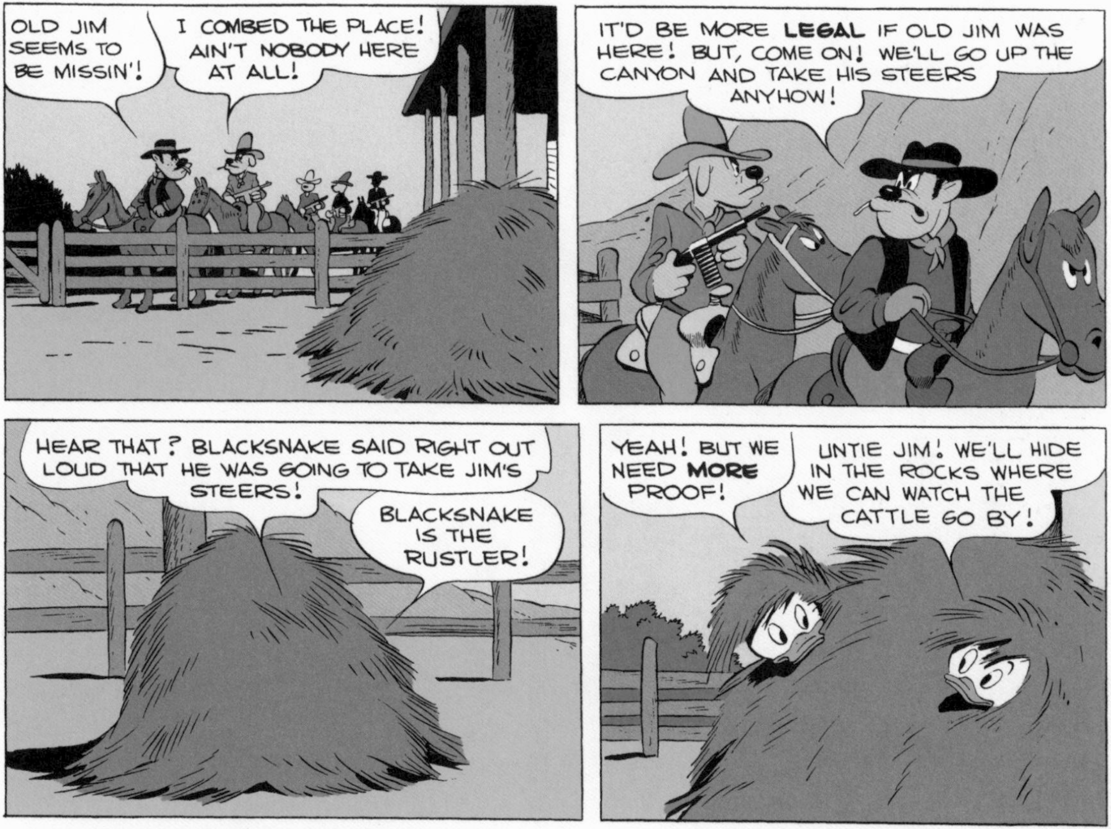
OLD JIM SEEMS TO BE MISSIN'!
I COMBED THE PLACE! AIN'T NOBODY HERE AT ALL!
IT'D BE MORE LEGAL IF OLD JIM WAS HERE! BUT, COME ON! WE'LL GO UP THE CANYON AND TAKE HIS STEERS ANYHOW!
HEAR THAT? BLACKSNAKE SAID RIGHT OUT LOUD THAT HE WAS GOING TO TAKE JIM'S STEERS!
BLACKSNAKE IS THE RUSTLER!
YEAH! BUT WE NEED MORE PROOF!
UNTIE JIM! WE'LL HIDE IN THE ROCKS WHERE WE CAN WATCH THE CATTLE GO BY!

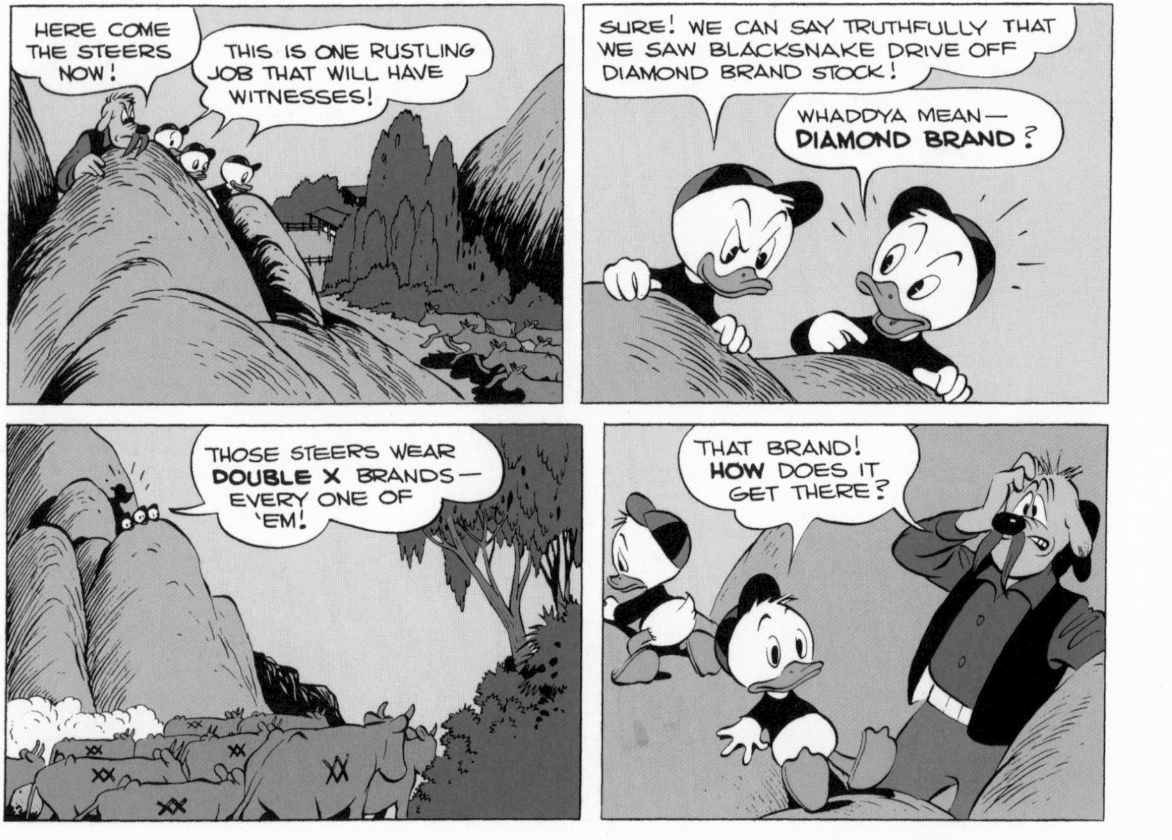
HERE COME THE STEERS NOW!
THIS IS ONE RUSTLING JOB THAT WILL HAVE WITNESSES!
SURE! WE CAN SAY TRUTHFULLY THAT WE SAW BLACKSNAKE DRIVE OFF DIAMOND BRAND STOCK!
WHADDYA MEAN— DIAMOND BRAND?
THOSE STEERS WEAR DOUBLE X BRANDS— EVERY ONE OF 'EM!
THAT BRAND! HOW DOES IT GET THERE?

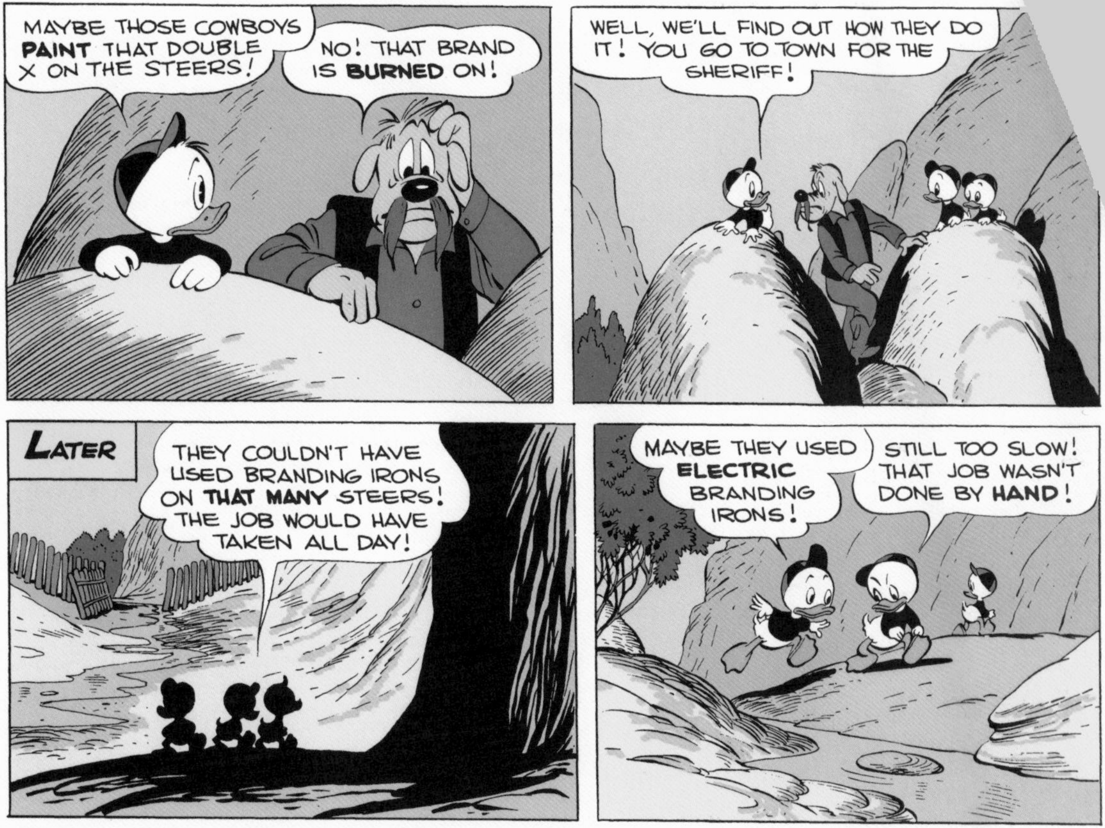
MAYBE THOSE COWBOYS PAINT THAT DOUBLE X ON THE STEERS!
NO! THAT BRAND IS BURNED ON!
WELL, WE'LL FIND OUT HOW THEY DO IT! YOU GO TO TOWN FOR THE SHERIFF!
LATER
THEY COULDN'T HAVE USED BRANDING IRONS ON THAT MANY STEERS! THE JOB WOULD HAVE TAKEN ALL DAY!
MAYBE THEY USED ELECTRIC BRANDING IRONS!
STILL TOO SLOW! THAT JOB WASN'T DONE BY HAND!

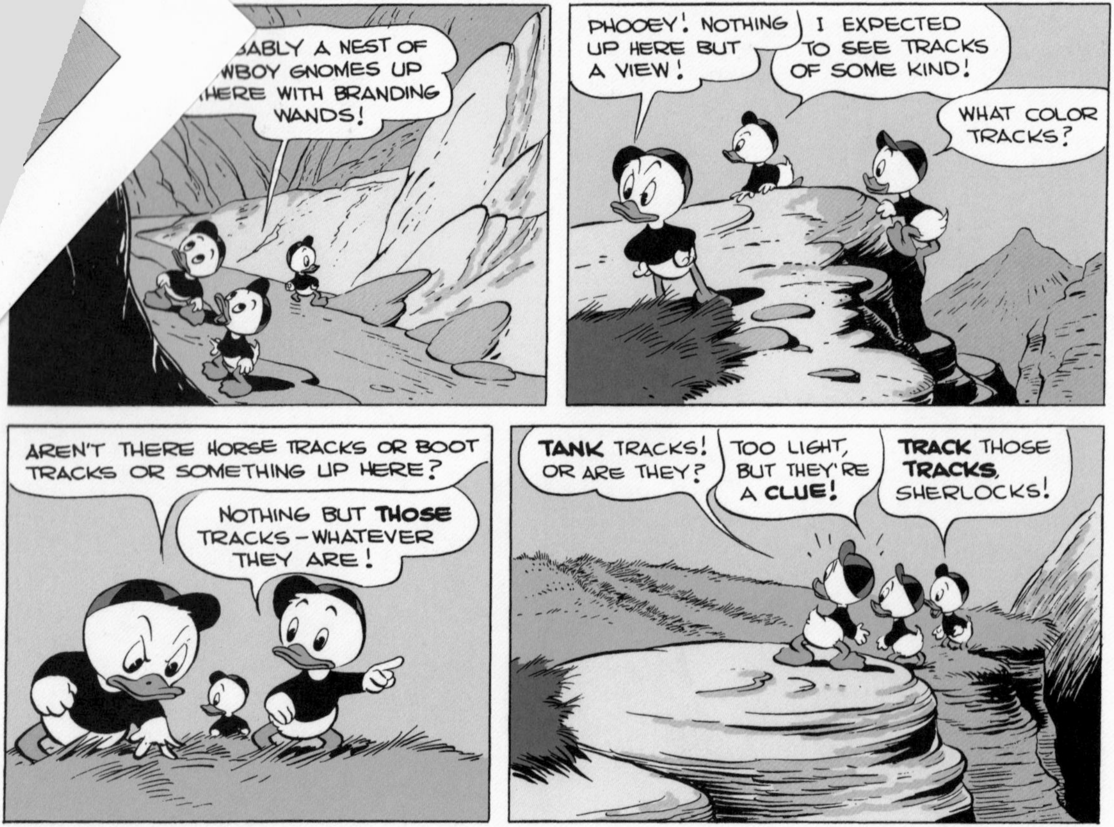
BABLY A NEST OF
WBOY GNOMES UP
HERE WITH BRANDING
WANDS!
PHOOEY! NOTHING UP HERE BUT A VIEW!
I EXPECTED TO SEE TRACKS OF SOME KIND!
WHAT COLOR TRACKS?
AREN'T THERE HORSE TRACKS OR BOOT TRACKS OR SOMETHING UP HERE?
NOTHING BUT **THOSE** TRACKS—WHATEVER THEY ARE!
TANK TRACKS! OR ARE THEY?
TOO LIGHT, BUT THEY'RE A **CLUE**!
TRACK THOSE **TRACKS**, SHERLOCKS!

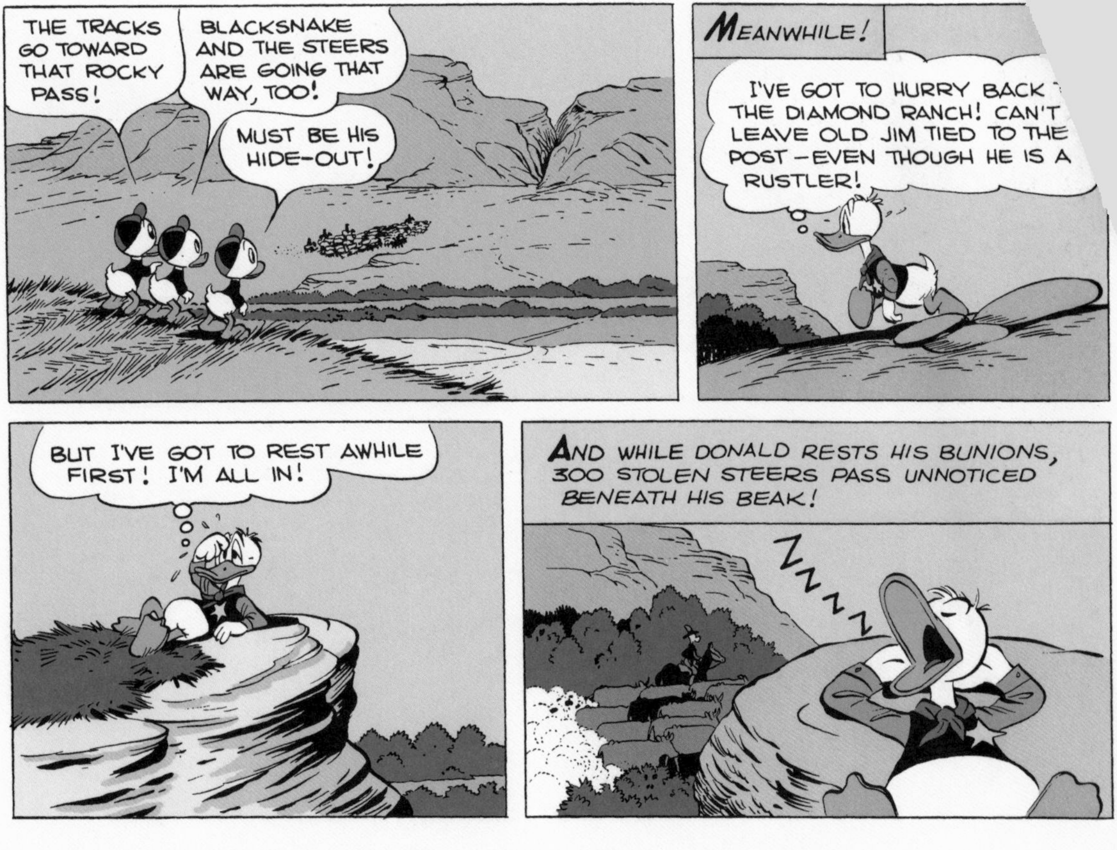
THE TRACKS GO TOWARD THAT ROCKY PASS!
BLACKSNAKE AND THE STEERS ARE GOING THAT WAY, TOO!
MUST BE HIS HIDE-OUT!
MEANWHILE!
I'VE GOT TO HURRY BACK THE DIAMOND RANCH! CAN'T LEAVE OLD JIM TIED TO THE POST—EVEN THOUGH HE IS A RUSTLER!
BUT I'VE GOT TO REST AWHILE FIRST! I'M ALL IN!
AND WHILE DONALD RESTS HIS BUNIONS, 300 STOLEN STEERS PASS UNNOTICED BENEATH HIS BEAK!
ZZZZ

...SES ON HIS WAY TO ...F!

ZZZZZ

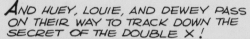

AND HUEY, LOUIE, AND DEWEY PASS ON THEIR WAY TO TRACK DOWN THE SECRET OF THE DOUBLE X!

ZZZ

WATCH OUT FOR THAT PASS! IT LOOKS LIKE A TRAP FULL OF POISONED LEAD!

WE'LL CLIMB OVER THE RIDGE TO THE SIDE! KEEP YOUR HEADS DOWN IF YOU WANT TO KEEP THEM ON!

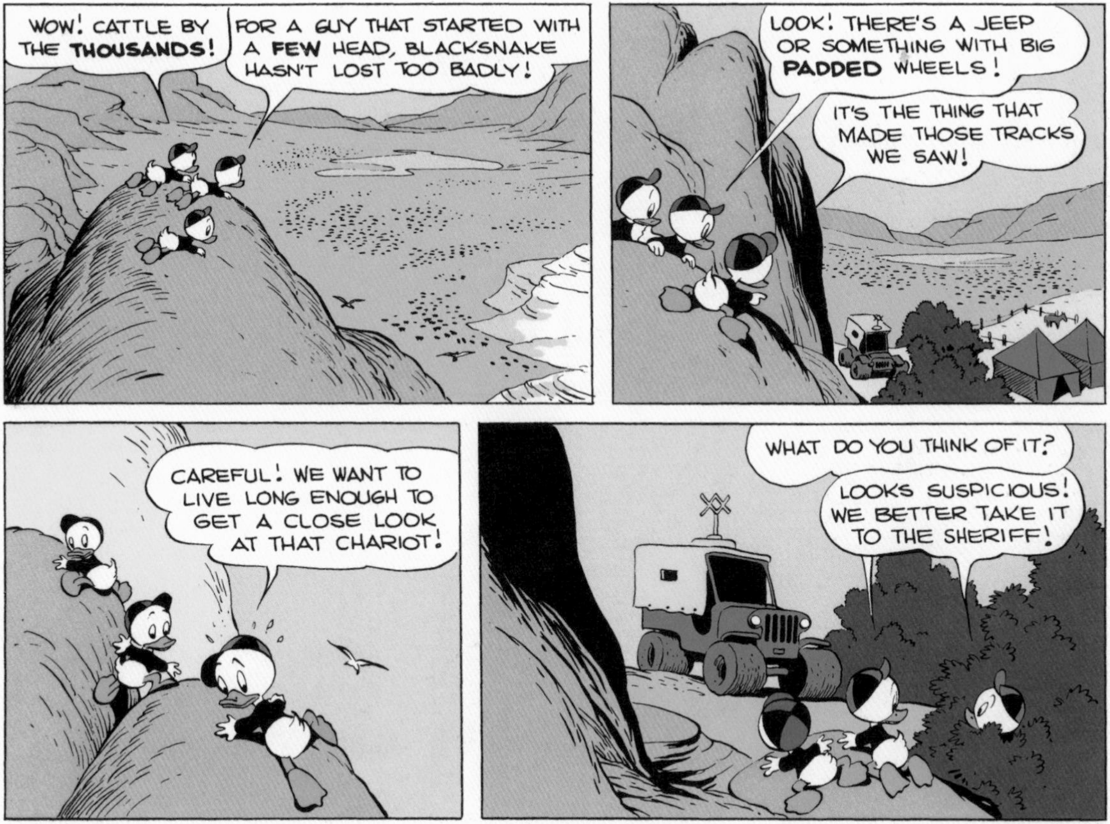
WOW! CATTLE BY THE **THOUSANDS**!
FOR A GUY THAT STARTED WITH A **FEW** HEAD, BLACKSNAKE HASN'T LOST TOO BADLY!
LOOK! THERE'S A JEEP OR SOMETHING WITH BIG **PADDED** WHEELS!
IT'S THE THING THAT MADE THOSE TRACKS WE SAW!
CAREFUL! WE WANT TO LIVE LONG ENOUGH TO GET A CLOSE LOOK AT THAT CHARIOT!
WHAT DO YOU THINK OF IT?
LOOKS SUSPICIOUS! WE BETTER TAKE IT TO THE SHERIFF!

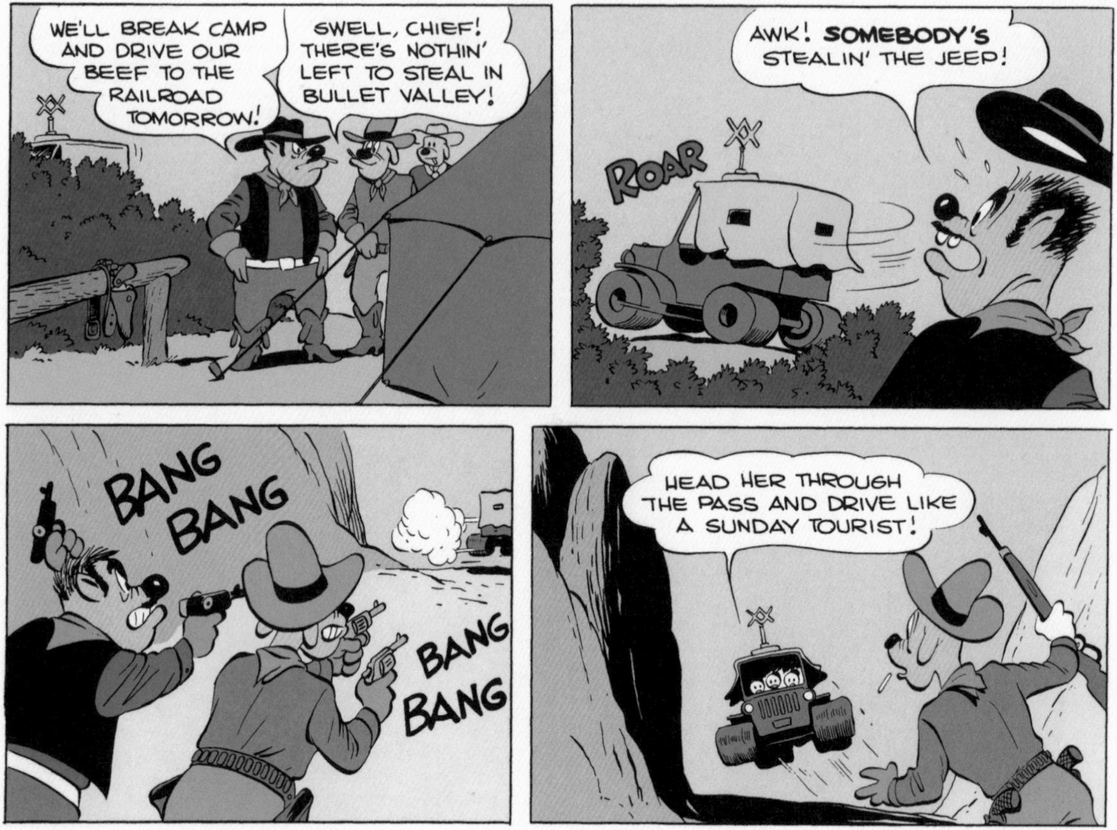
WE'LL BREAK CAMP AND DRIVE OUR BEEF TO THE RAILROAD TOMORROW!
SWELL, CHIEF! THERE'S NOTHIN' LEFT TO STEAL IN BULLET VALLEY!
ROAR
AWK! SOMEBODY'S STEALIN' THE JEEP!
BANG BANG
BANG BANG
HEAD HER THROUGH THE PASS AND DRIVE LIKE A SUNDAY TOURIST!

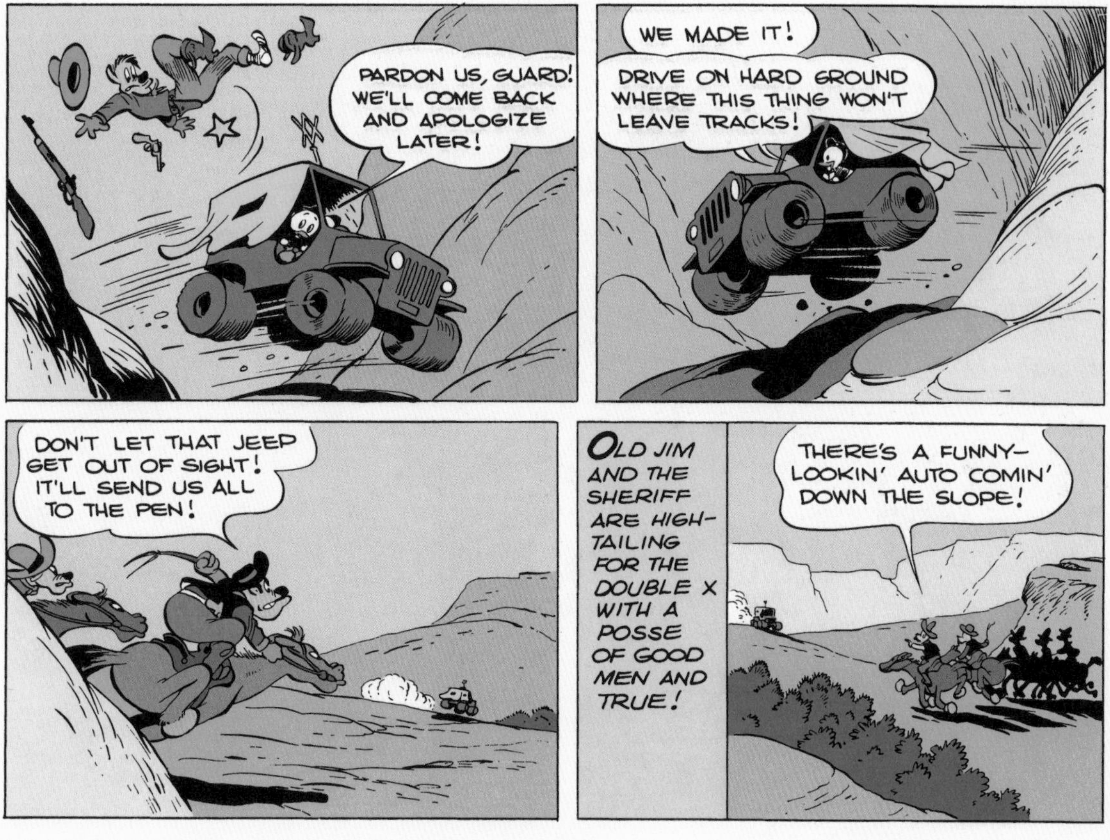
PARDON US, GUARD! WE'LL COME BACK AND APOLOGIZE LATER!
WE MADE IT!
DRIVE ON HARD GROUND WHERE THIS THING WON'T LEAVE TRACKS!
DON'T LET THAT JEEP GET OUT OF SIGHT! IT'LL SEND US ALL TO THE PEN!
OLD JIM AND THE SHERIFF ARE HIGH-TAILING FOR THE DOUBLE X WITH A POSSE OF GOOD MEN AND TRUE!
THERE'S A FUNNY-LOOKIN' AUTO COMIN' DOWN THE SLOPE!

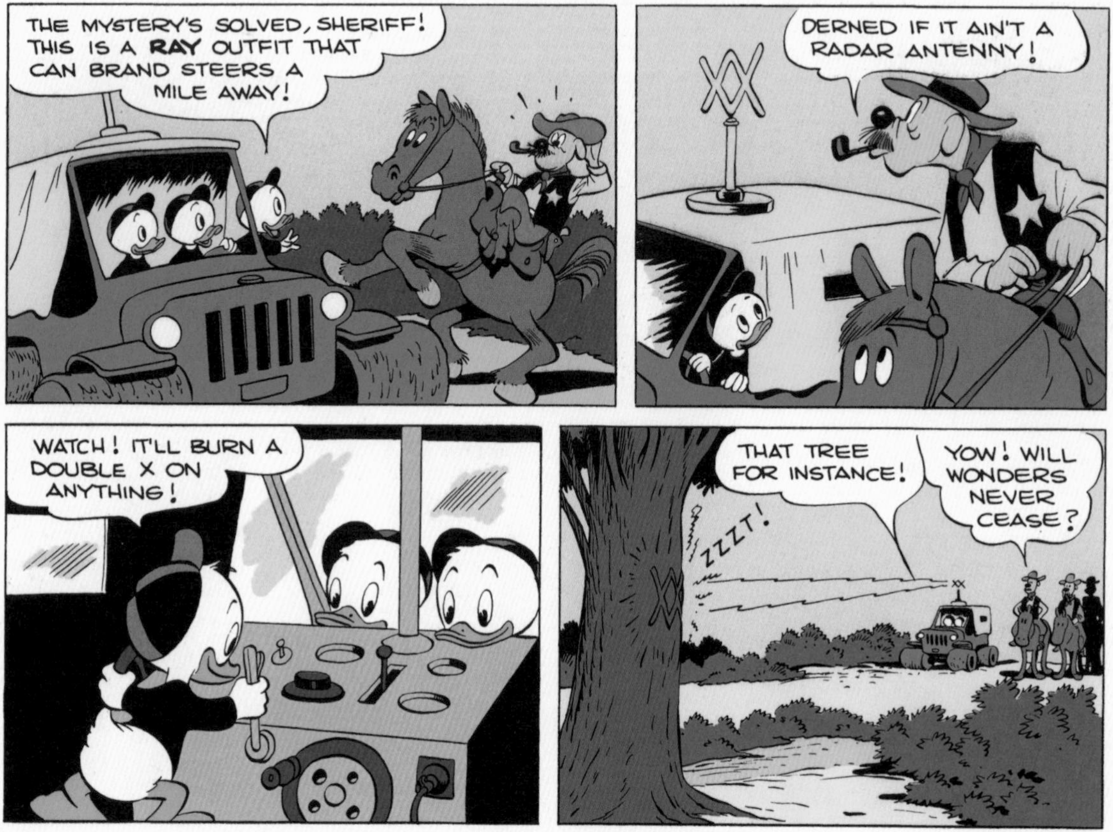

THE MYSTERY'S SOLVED, SHERIFF! THIS IS A **RAY** OUTFIT THAT CAN BRAND STEERS A MILE AWAY!
DERNED IF IT AIN'T A RADAR ANTENNY!
WATCH! IT'LL BURN A DOUBLE X ON ANYTHING!
THAT TREE FOR INSTANCE!
YOW! WILL WONDERS NEVER CEASE?
ZZZT!

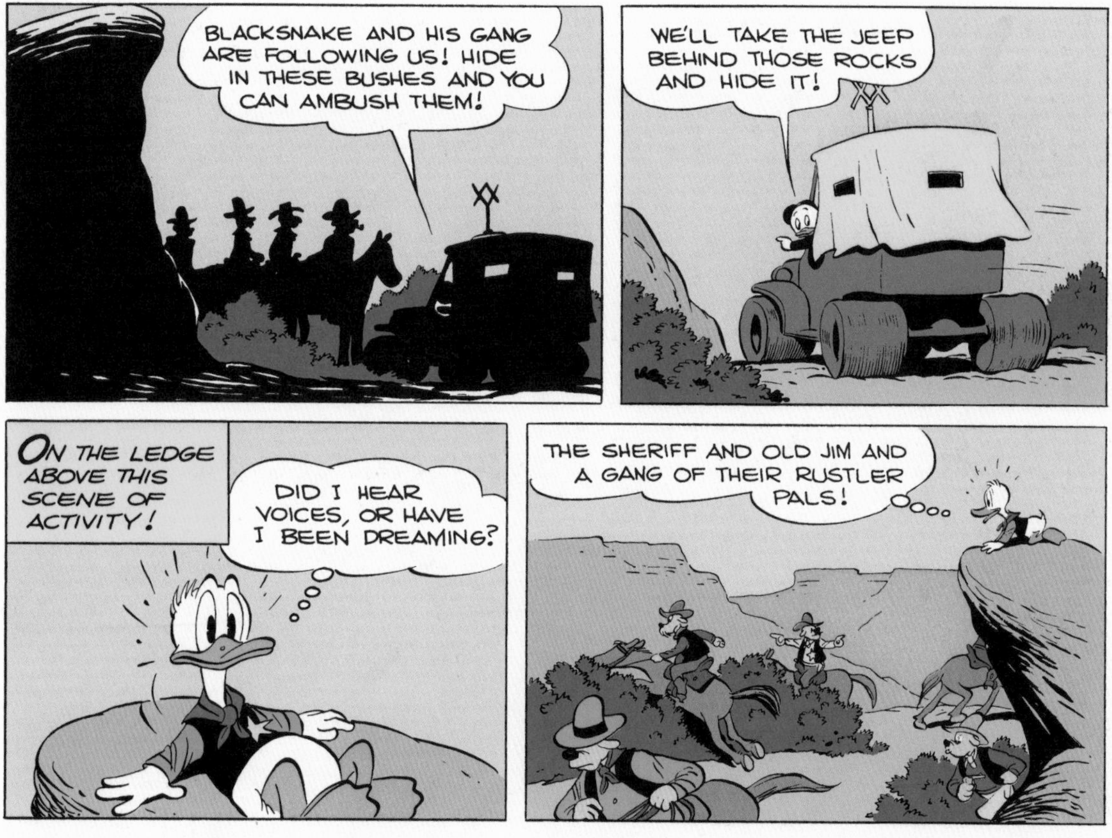
BLACKSNAKE AND HIS GANG ARE FOLLOWING US! HIDE IN THESE BUSHES AND YOU CAN AMBUSH THEM!
WE'LL TAKE THE JEEP BEHIND THOSE ROCKS AND HIDE IT!
ON THE LEDGE ABOVE THIS SCENE OF ACTIVITY!
DID I HEAR VOICES, OR HAVE I BEEN DREAMING?
THE SHERIFF AND OLD JIM AND A GANG OF THEIR RUSTLER PALS!

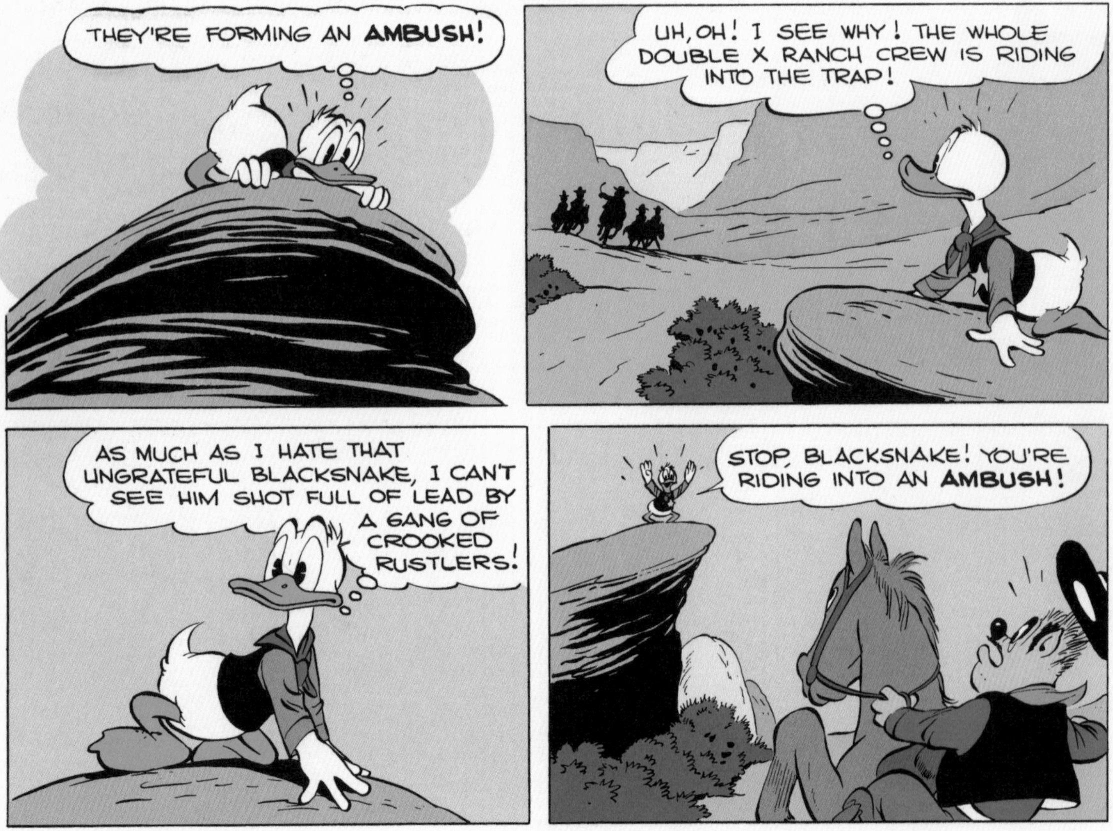
THEY'RE FORMING AN **AMBUSH**!
UH, OH! I SEE WHY! THE WHOLE DOUBLE X RANCH CREW IS RIDING INTO THE TRAP!
AS MUCH AS I HATE THAT UNGRATEFUL BLACKSNAKE, I CAN'T SEE HIM SHOT FULL OF LEAD BY A GANG OF CROOKED RUSTLERS!
STOP, BLACKSNAKE! YOU'RE RIDING INTO AN **AMBUSH**!

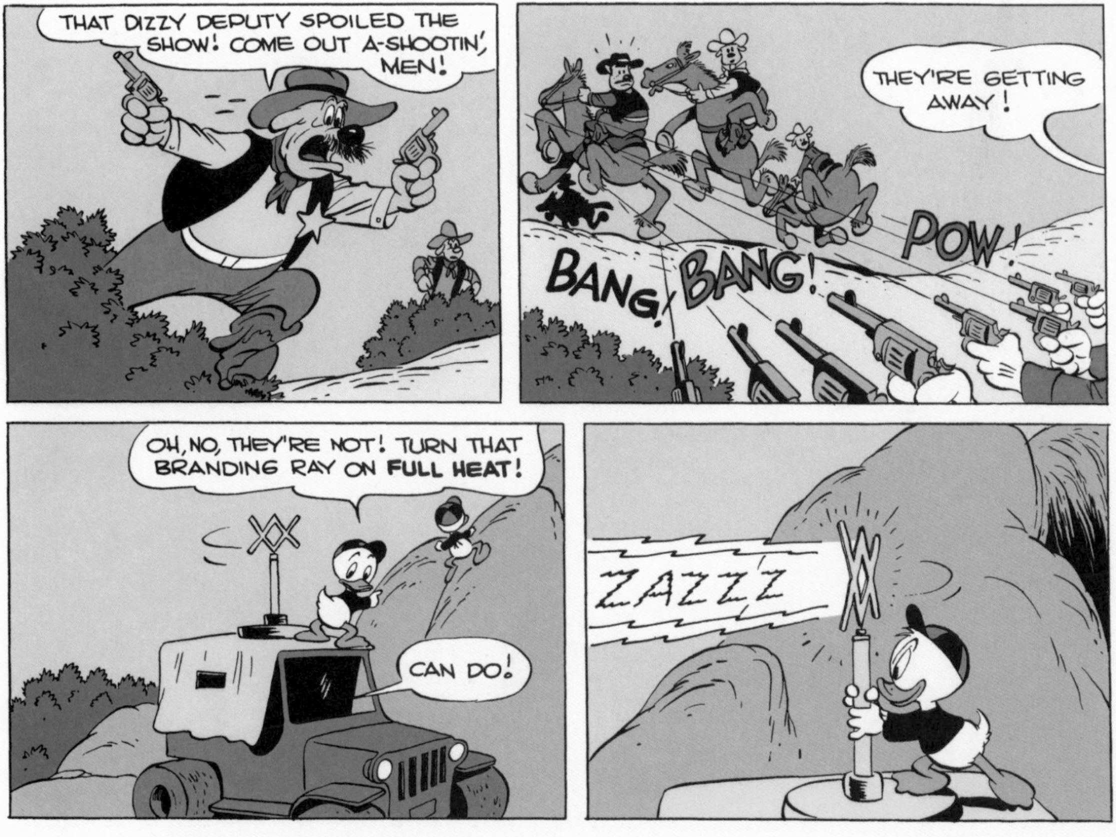
THAT DIZZY DEPUTY SPOILED THE SHOW! COME OUT A-SHOOTIN', MEN!
THEY'RE GETTING AWAY!
BANG!
BANG!
POW!
OH, NO, THEY'RE NOT! TURN THAT BRANDING RAY ON **FULL HEAT**!
CAN DO!
ZAZZZ

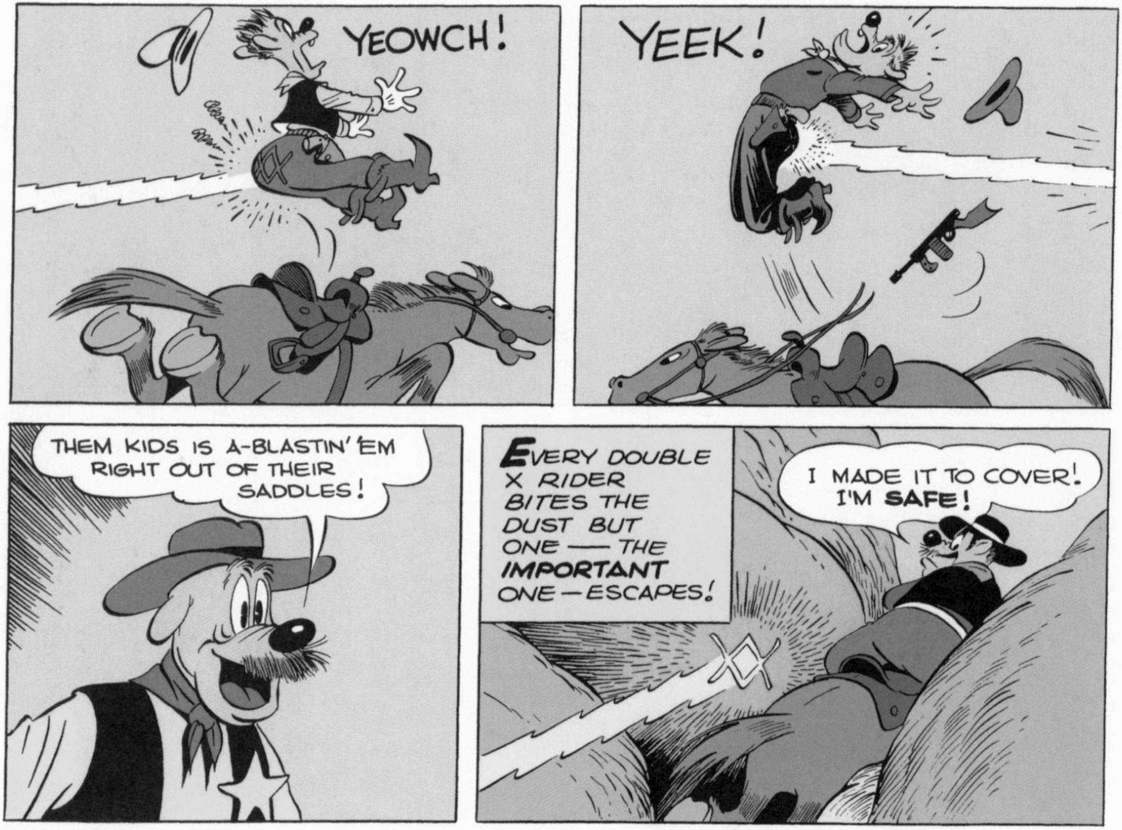
YEOWCH!
YEEK!
THEM KIDS IS A-BLASTIN' 'EM RIGHT OUT OF THEIR SADDLES!
EVERY DOUBLE X RIDER BITES THE DUST BUT ONE — THE **IMPORTANT** ONE—ESCAPES!
I MADE IT TO COVER! I'M **SAFE**!

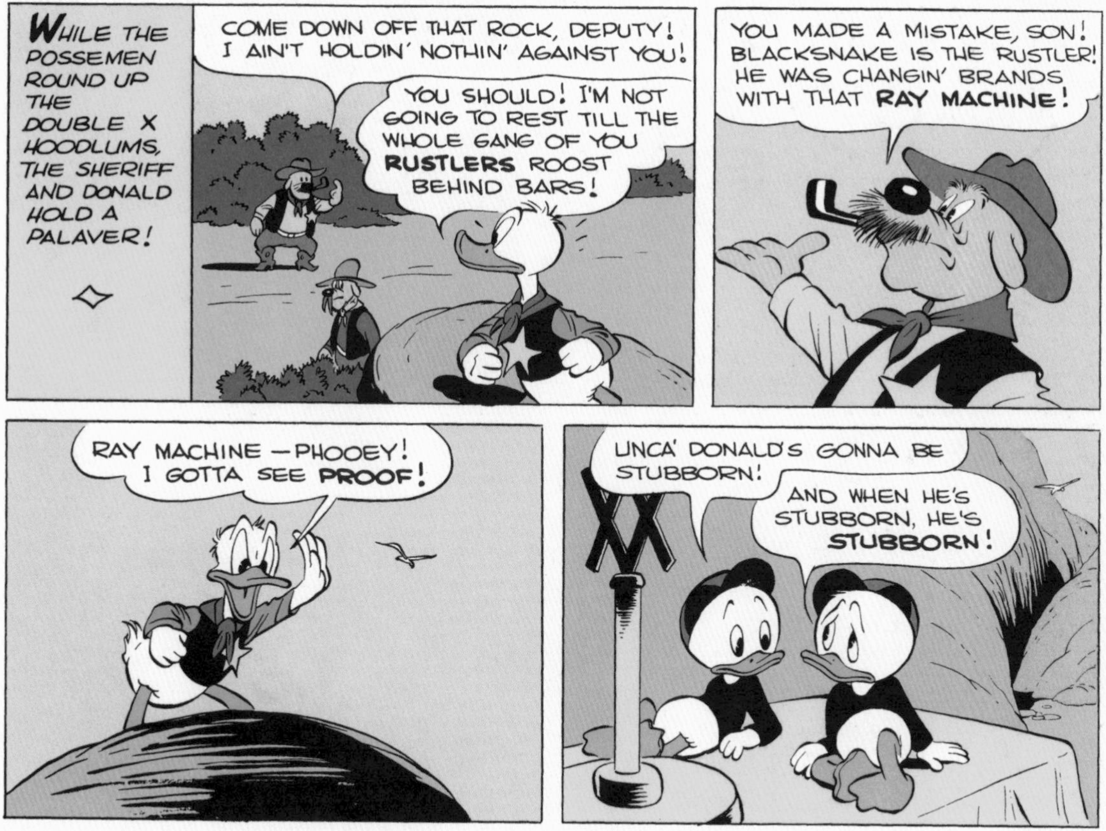

WHILE THE POSSEMEN ROUND UP THE DOUBLE X HOODLUMS, THE SHERIFF AND DONALD HOLD A PALAVER!
COME DOWN OFF THAT ROCK, DEPUTY! I AIN'T HOLDIN' NOTHIN' AGAINST YOU!
YOU SHOULD! I'M NOT GOING TO REST TILL THE WHOLE GANG OF YOU RUSTLERS ROOST BEHIND BARS!
YOU MADE A MISTAKE, SON! BLACKSNAKE IS THE RUSTLER! HE WAS CHANGIN' BRANDS WITH THAT RAY MACHINE!
RAY MACHINE — PHOOEY! I GOTTA SEE PROOF!
UNCA' DONALD'S GONNA BE STUBBORN!
AND WHEN HE'S STUBBORN, HE'S STUBBORN!

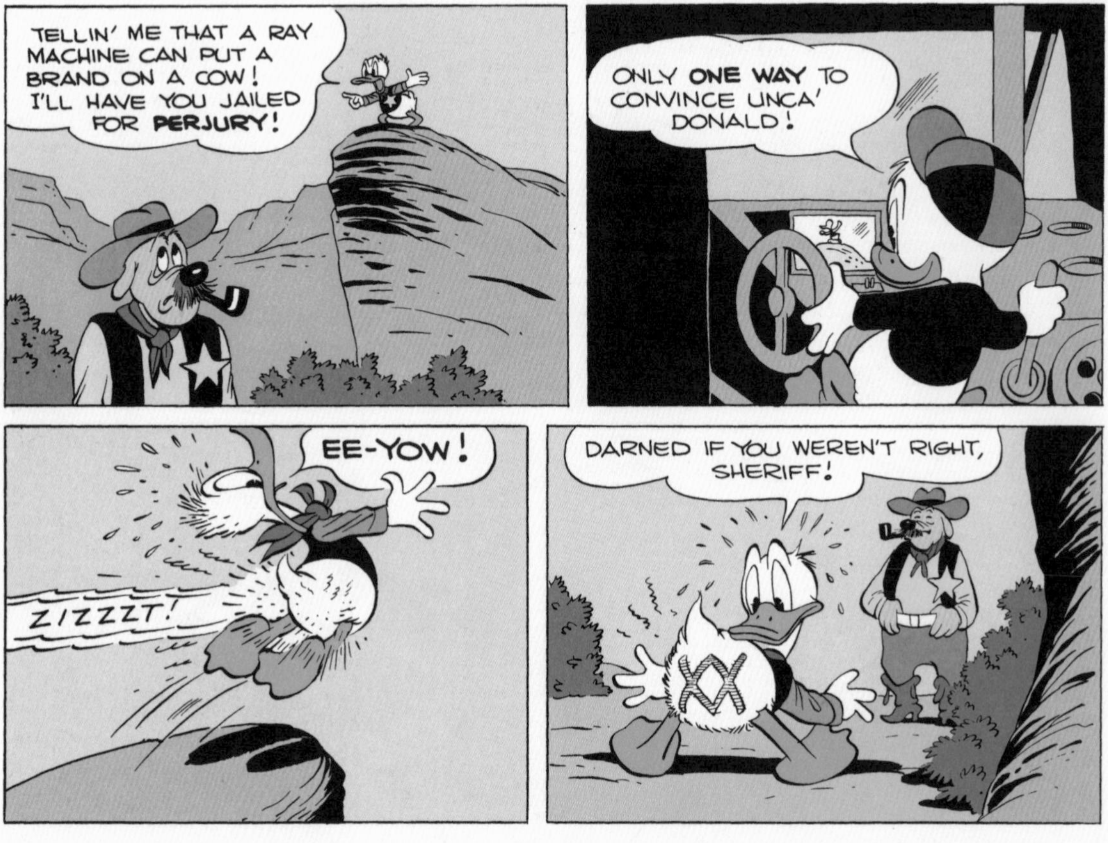
TELLIN' ME THAT A RAY MACHINE CAN PUT A BRAND ON A COW! I'LL HAVE YOU JAILED FOR **PERJURY**!
ONLY **ONE WAY** TO CONVINCE UNCA' DONALD!
EE-YOW!
ZIZZZT!
DARNED IF YOU WEREN'T RIGHT, SHERIFF!

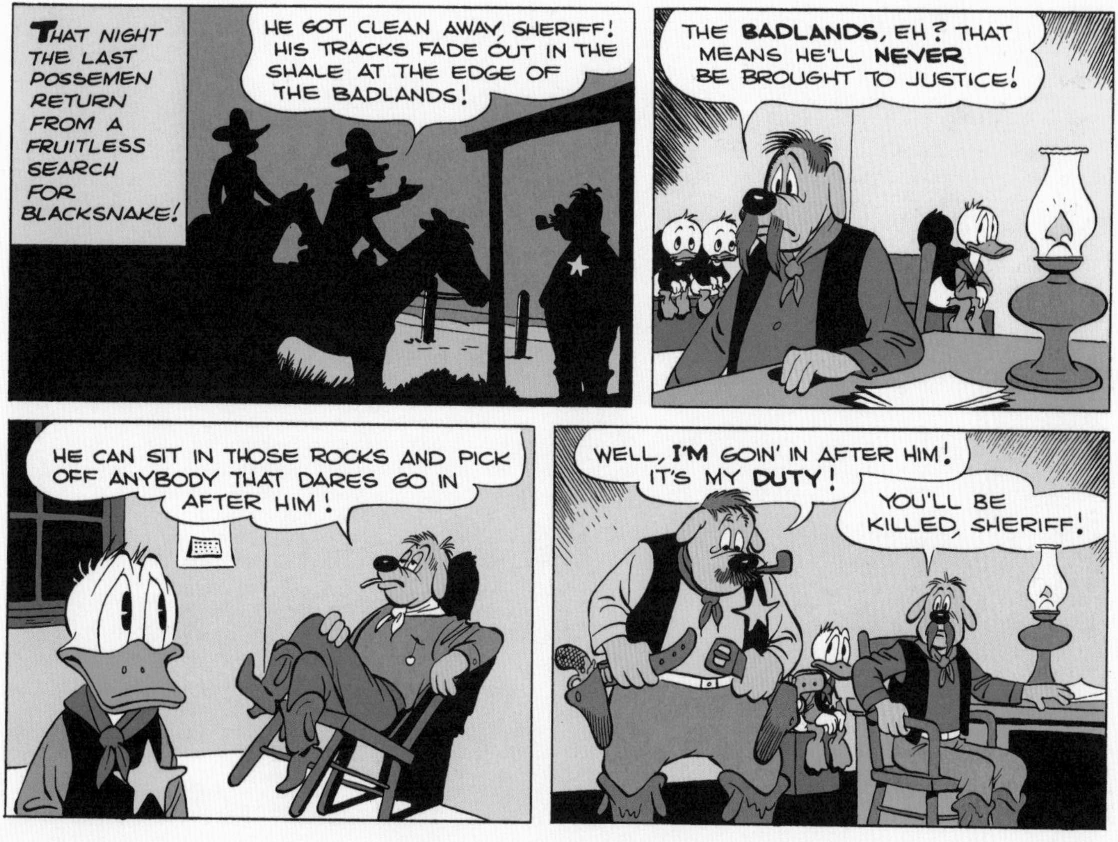
THAT NIGHT THE LAST POSSEMEN RETURN FROM A FRUITLESS SEARCH FOR BLACKSNAKE!
HE GOT CLEAN AWAY, SHERIFF! HIS TRACKS FADE OUT IN THE SHALE AT THE EDGE OF THE BADLANDS!
THE **BADLANDS**, EH? THAT MEANS HE'LL **NEVER** BE BROUGHT TO JUSTICE!
HE CAN SIT IN THOSE ROCKS AND PICK OFF ANYBODY THAT DARES GO IN AFTER HIM!
WELL, **I'M** GOIN' IN AFTER HIM! IT'S MY **DUTY**!
YOU'LL BE KILLED, SHERIFF!

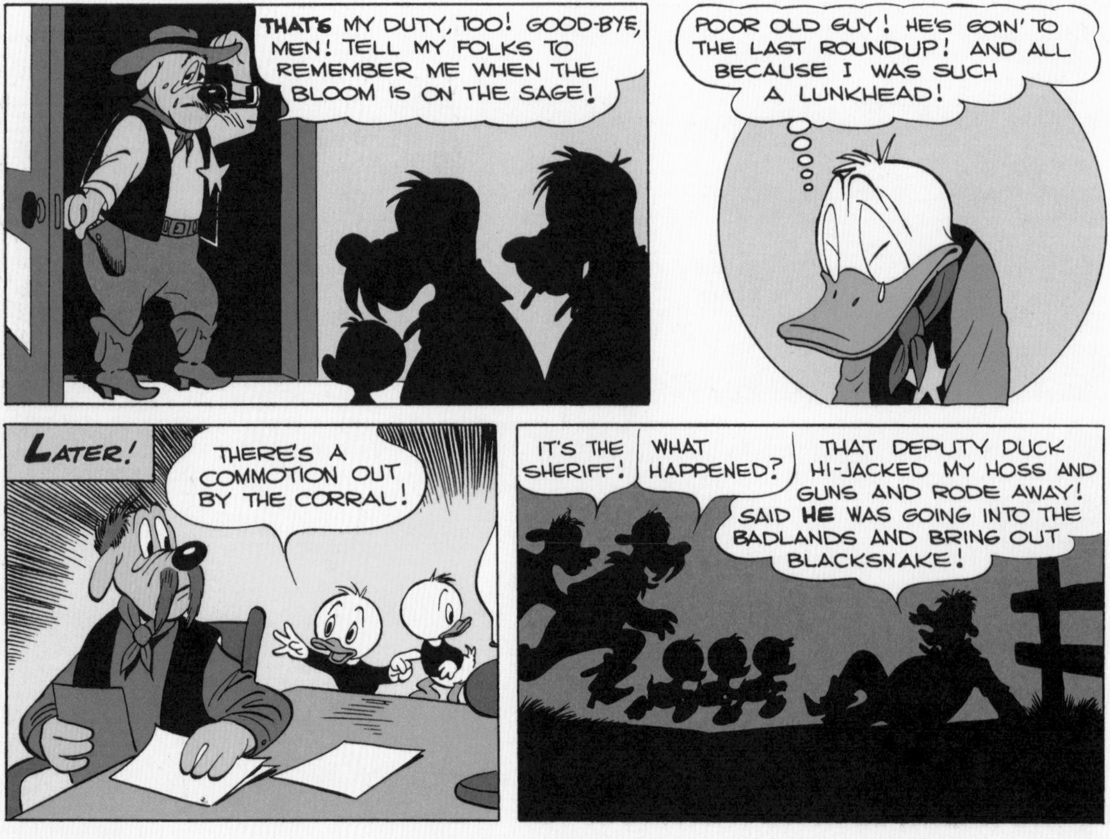

THAT'S MY DUTY, TOO! GOOD-BYE, MEN! TELL MY FOLKS TO REMEMBER ME WHEN THE BLOOM IS ON THE SAGE!
POOR OLD GUY! HE'S GOIN' TO THE LAST ROUNDUP! AND ALL BECAUSE I WAS SUCH A LUNKHEAD!
LATER!
THERE'S A COMMOTION OUT BY THE CORRAL!
IT'S THE SHERIFF!
WHAT HAPPENED?
THAT DEPUTY DUCK HI-JACKED MY HOSS AND GUNS AND RODE AWAY! SAID HE WAS GOING INTO THE BADLANDS AND BRING OUT BLACKSNAKE!

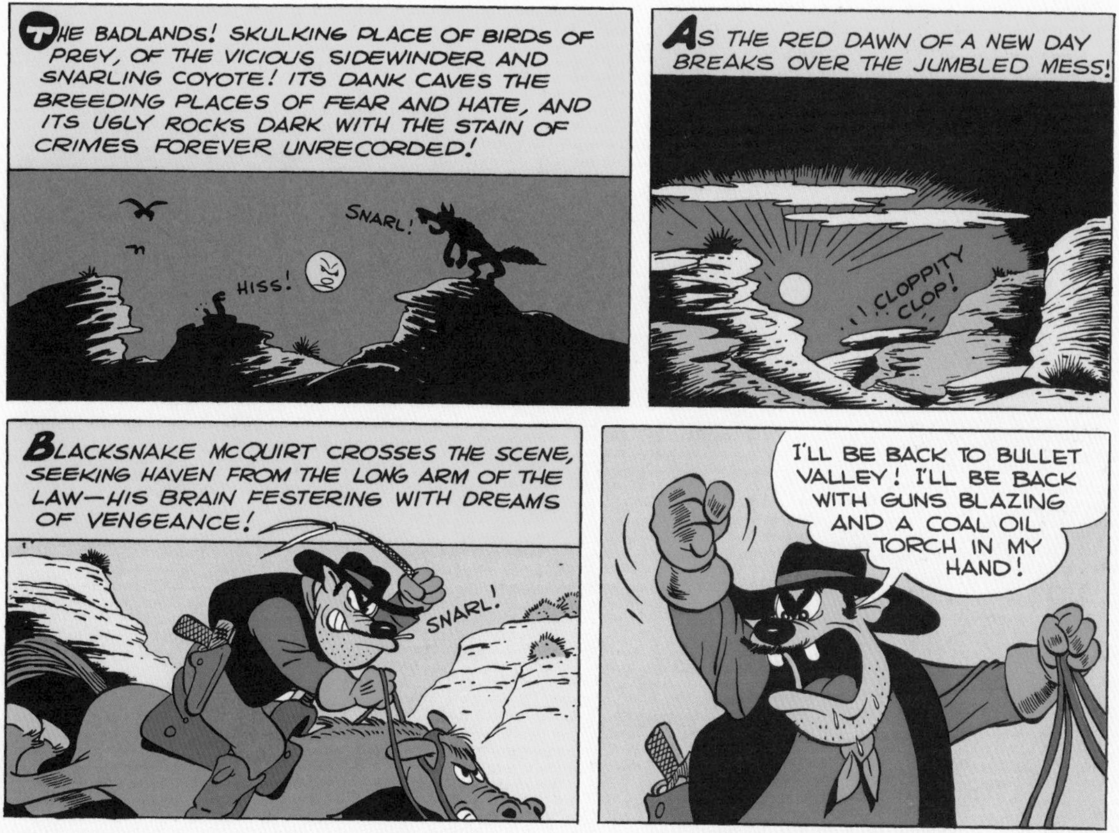
THE BADLANDS! SKULKING PLACE OF BIRDS OF PREY, OF THE VICIOUS SIDEWINDER AND SNARLING COYOTE! ITS DANK CAVES THE BREEDING PLACES OF FEAR AND HATE, AND ITS UGLY ROCKS DARK WITH THE STAIN OF CRIMES FOREVER UNRECORDED!
SNARL!
HISS!
AS THE RED DAWN OF A NEW DAY BREAKS OVER THE JUMBLED MESS!
CLOPPITY CLOP!
BLACKSNAKE McQUIRT CROSSES THE SCENE, SEEKING HAVEN FROM THE LONG ARM OF THE LAW—HIS BRAIN FESTERING WITH DREAMS OF VENGEANCE!
SNARL!
I'LL BE BACK TO BULLET VALLEY! I'LL BE BACK WITH GUNS BLAZING AND A COAL OIL TORCH IN MY HAND!

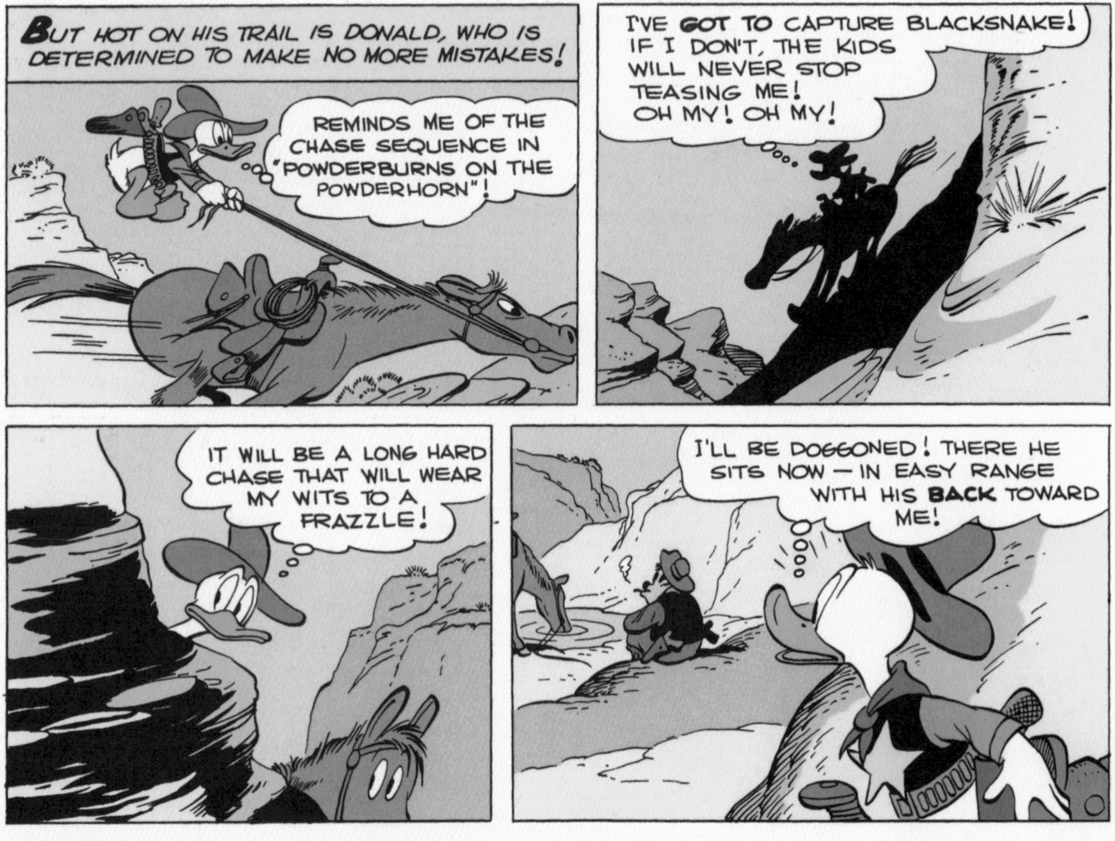
BUT HOT ON HIS TRAIL IS DONALD, WHO IS DETERMINED TO MAKE NO MORE MISTAKES!
REMINDS ME OF THE CHASE SEQUENCE IN "POWDERBURNS ON THE POWDERHORN"!
I'VE GOT TO CAPTURE BLACKSNAKE! IF I DON'T, THE KIDS WILL NEVER STOP TEASING ME! OH MY! OH MY!
IT WILL BE A LONG HARD CHASE THAT WILL WEAR MY WITS TO A FRAZZLE!
I'LL BE DOGGONED! THERE HE SITS NOW — IN EASY RANGE WITH HIS BACK TOWARD ME!

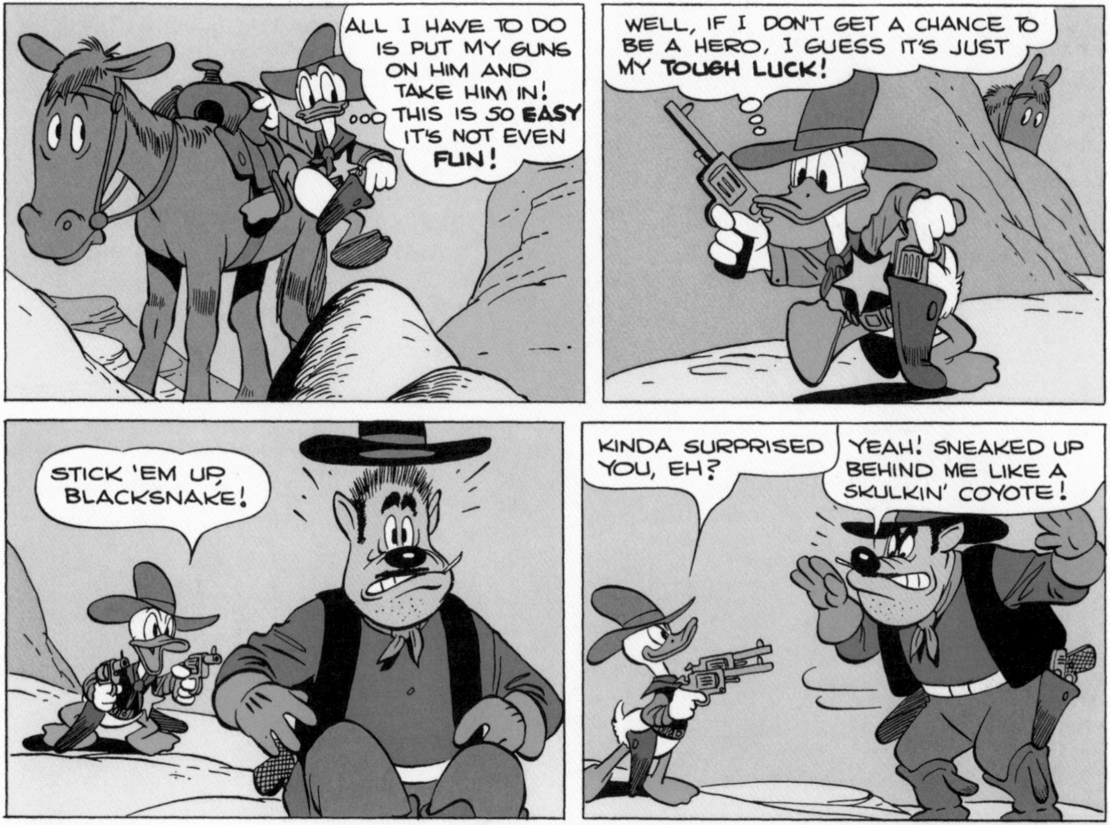
ALL I HAVE TO DO IS PUT MY GUNS ON HIM AND TAKE HIM IN! THIS IS SO EASY IT'S NOT EVEN FUN!
WELL, IF I DON'T GET A CHANCE TO BE A HERO, I GUESS IT'S JUST MY TOUGH LUCK!
STICK 'EM UP, BLACKSNAKE!
KINDA SURPRISED YOU, EH?
YEAH! SNEAKED UP BEHIND ME LIKE A SKULKIN' COYOTE!

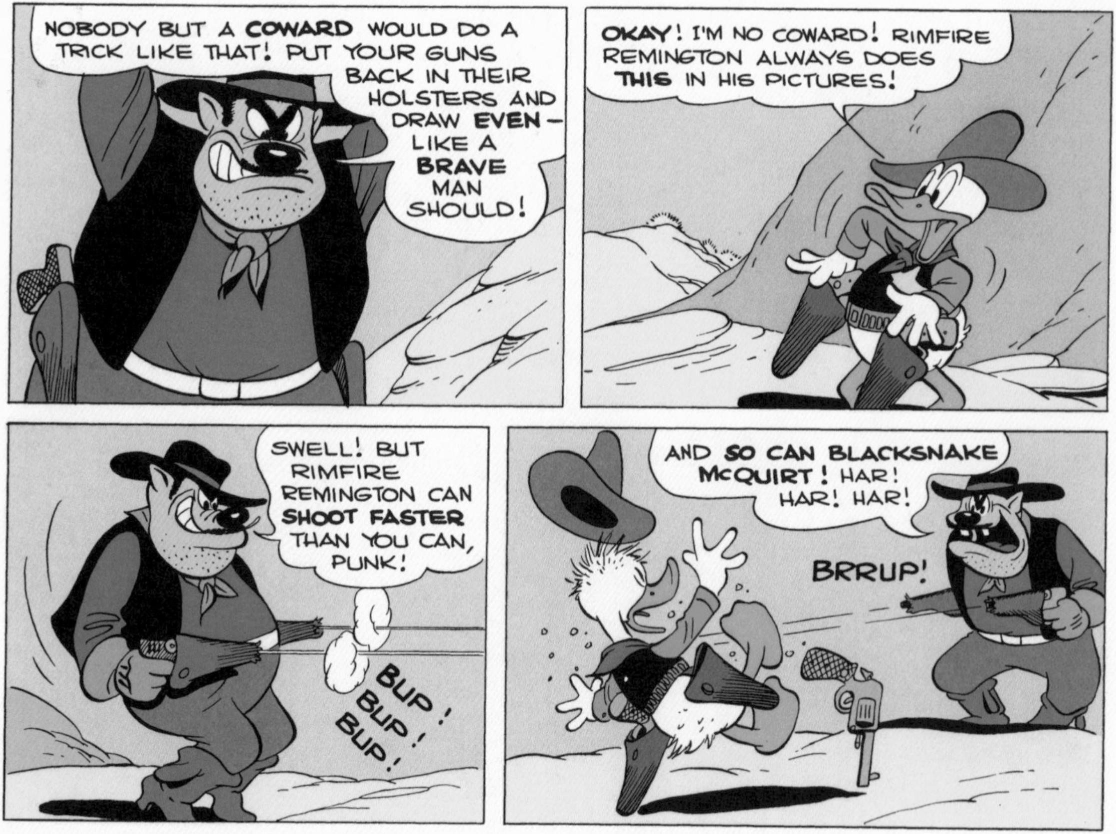
NOBODY BUT A COWARD WOULD DO A TRICK LIKE THAT! PUT YOUR GUNS BACK IN THEIR HOLSTERS AND DRAW EVEN — LIKE A BRAVE MAN SHOULD!
OKAY! I'M NO COWARD! RIMFIRE REMINGTON ALWAYS DOES THIS IN HIS PICTURES!
SWELL! BUT RIMFIRE REMINGTON CAN SHOOT FASTER THAN YOU CAN, PUNK!
BLIP! BLIP! BLIP!
AND SO CAN BLACKSNAKE McQUIRT! HAR! HAR! HAR!
BRRUP!

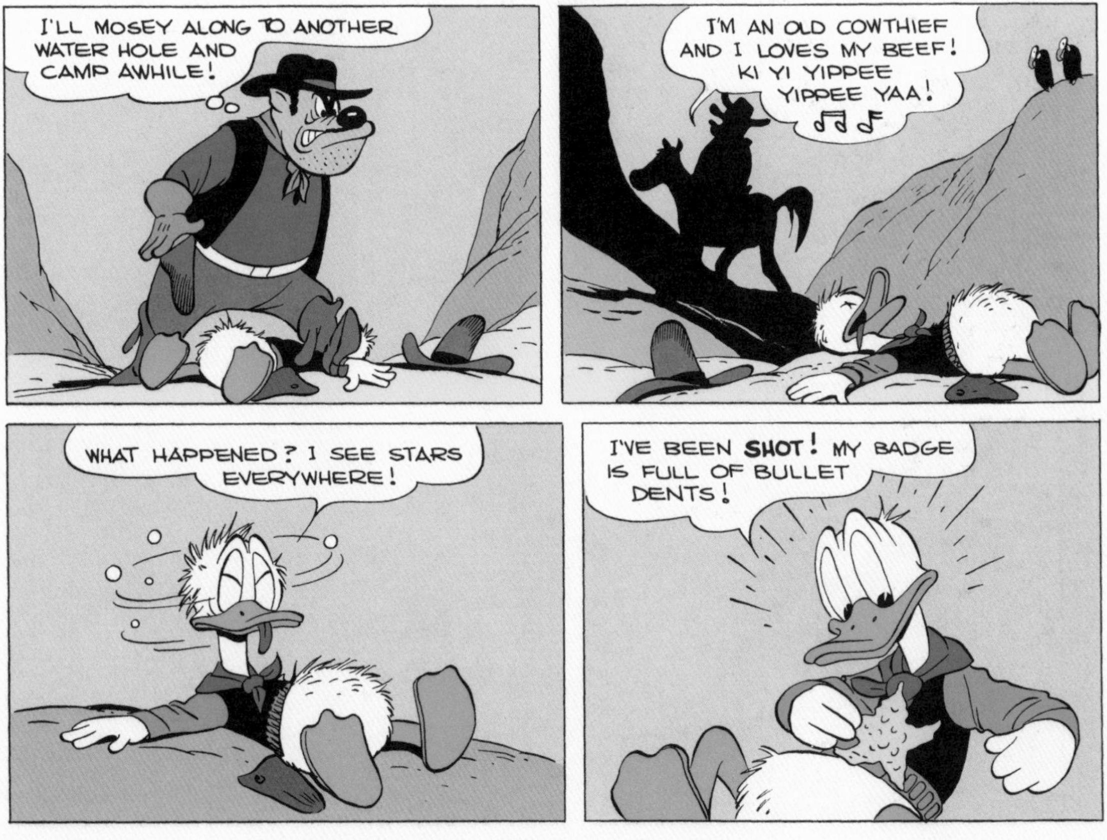
I'LL MOSEY ALONG TO ANOTHER WATER HOLE AND CAMP AWHILE!
I'M AN OLD COWTHIEF AND I LOVES MY BEEF! KI YI YIPPEE YIPPEE YAA!
WHAT HAPPENED? I SEE STARS EVERYWHERE!
I'VE BEEN SHOT! MY BADGE IS FULL OF BULLET DENTS!

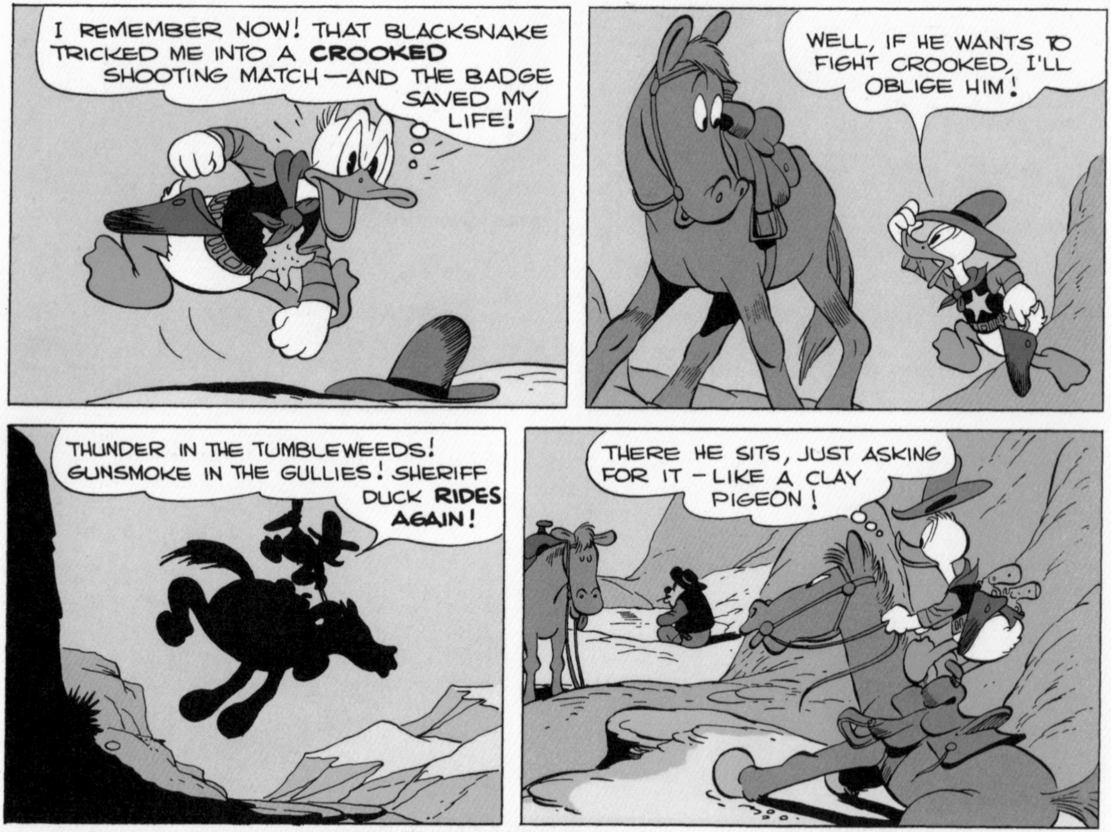
I REMEMBER NOW! THAT BLACKSNAKE TRICKED ME INTO A **CROOKED** SHOOTING MATCH—AND THE BADGE SAVED MY LIFE!
WELL, IF HE WANTS TO FIGHT CROOKED, I'LL OBLIGE HIM!
THUNDER IN THE TUMBLEWEEDS! GUNSMOKE IN THE GULLIES! SHERIFF DUCK **RIDES AGAIN**!
THERE HE SITS, JUST ASKING FOR IT - LIKE A CLAY PIGEON!

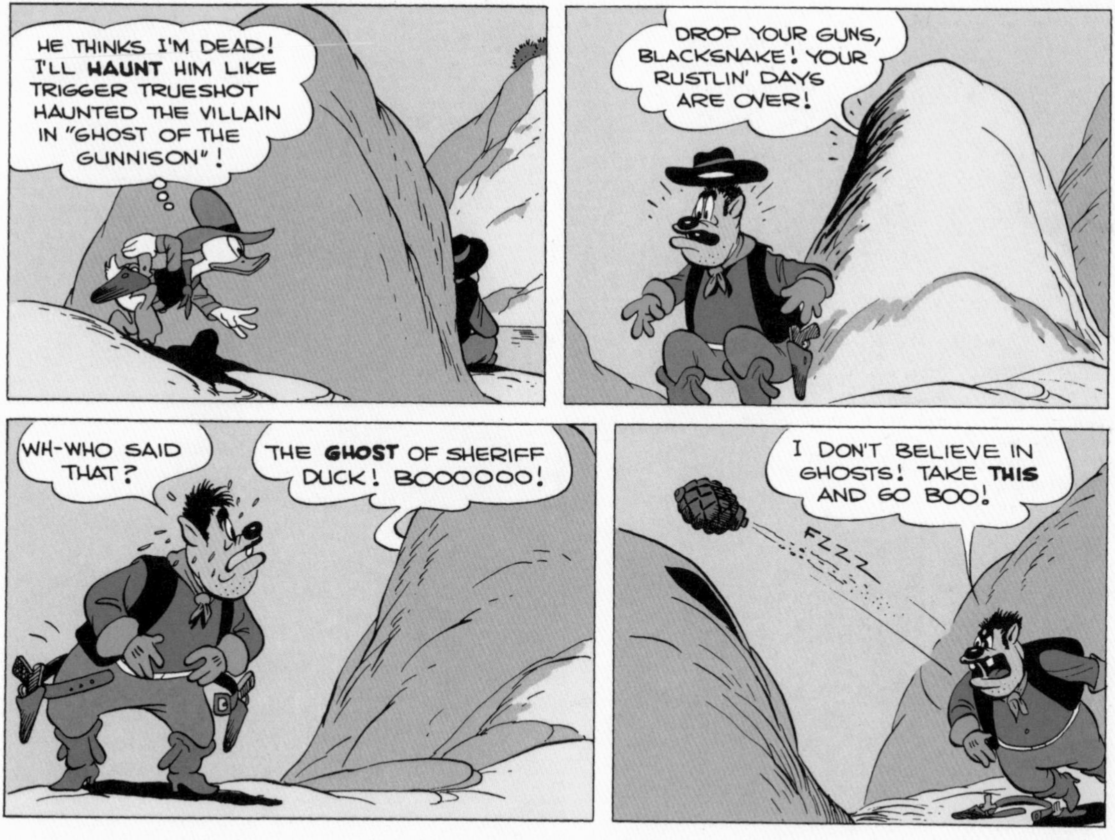
HE THINKS I'M DEAD! I'LL **HAUNT** HIM LIKE TRIGGER TRUESHOT HAUNTED THE VILLAIN IN "GHOST OF THE GUNNISON"!
DROP YOUR GUNS, BLACKSNAKE! YOUR RUSTLIN' DAYS ARE OVER!
WH-WHO SAID THAT?
THE **GHOST** OF SHERIFF DUCK! BOOOOOO!
I DON'T BELIEVE IN GHOSTS! TAKE **THIS** AND GO BOO!
FZZZ

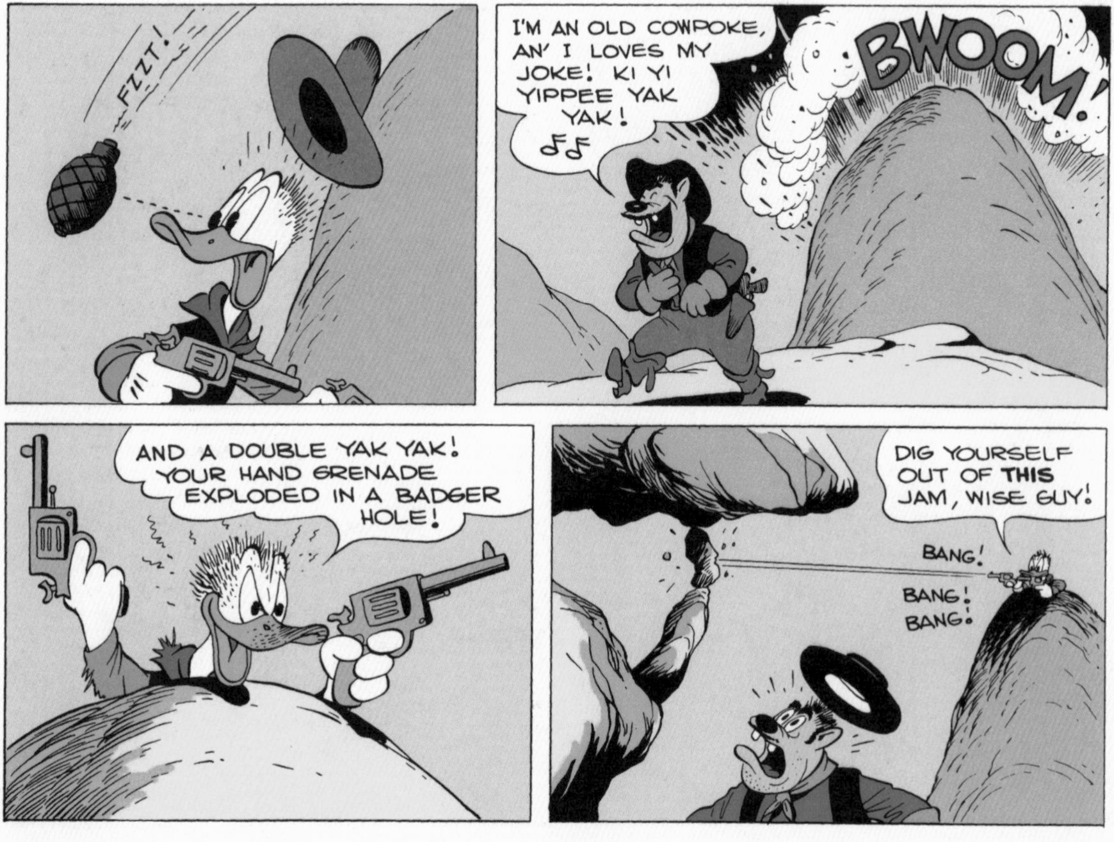
FZZT!
I'M AN OLD COWPOKE, AN' I LOVES MY JOKE! KI YI YIPPEE YAK YAK!
BWOOM!
AND A DOUBLE YAK YAK! YOUR HAND GRENADE EXPLODED IN A BADGER HOLE!
DIG YOURSELF OUT OF **THIS** JAM, WISE GUY!
BANG!
BANG!
BANG!

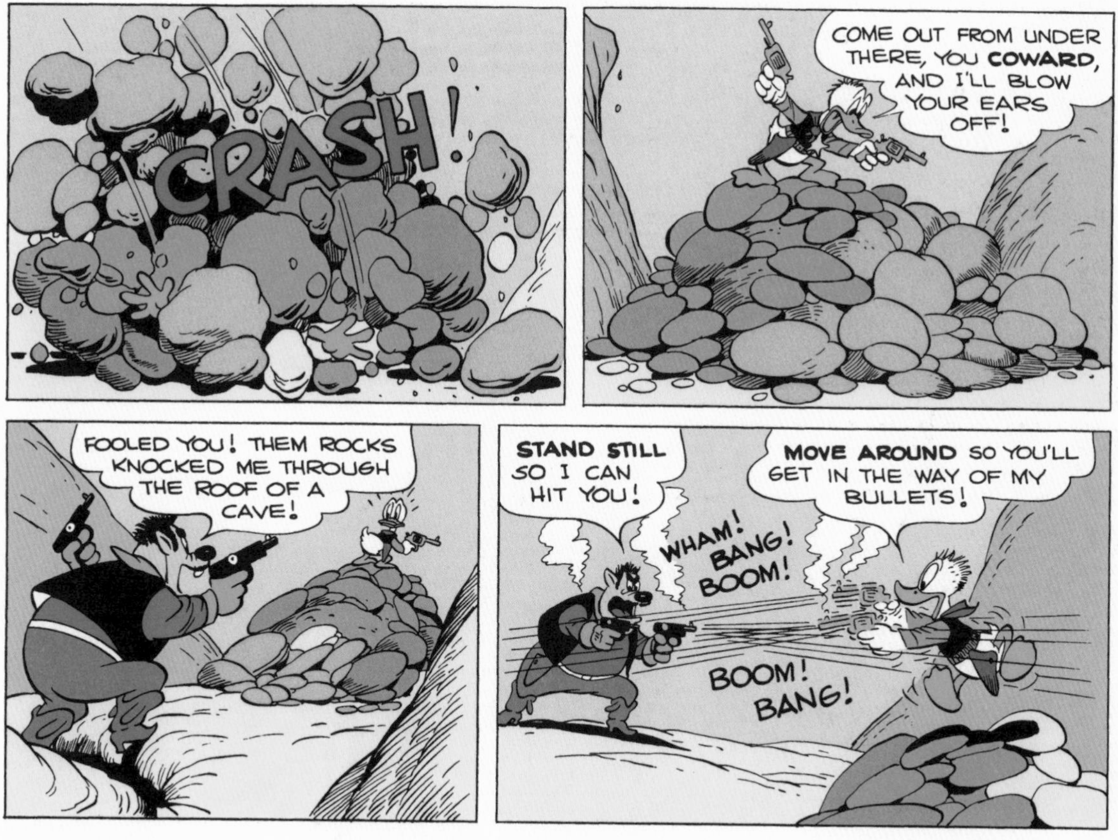
CRASH!
COME OUT FROM UNDER THERE, YOU **COWARD**, AND I'LL BLOW YOUR EARS OFF!
FOOLED YOU! THEM ROCKS KNOCKED ME THROUGH THE ROOF OF A CAVE!
STAND STILL SO I CAN HIT YOU!
MOVE AROUND SO YOU'LL GET IN THE WAY OF MY BULLETS!
WHAM! BANG! BOOM!
BOOM! BANG!

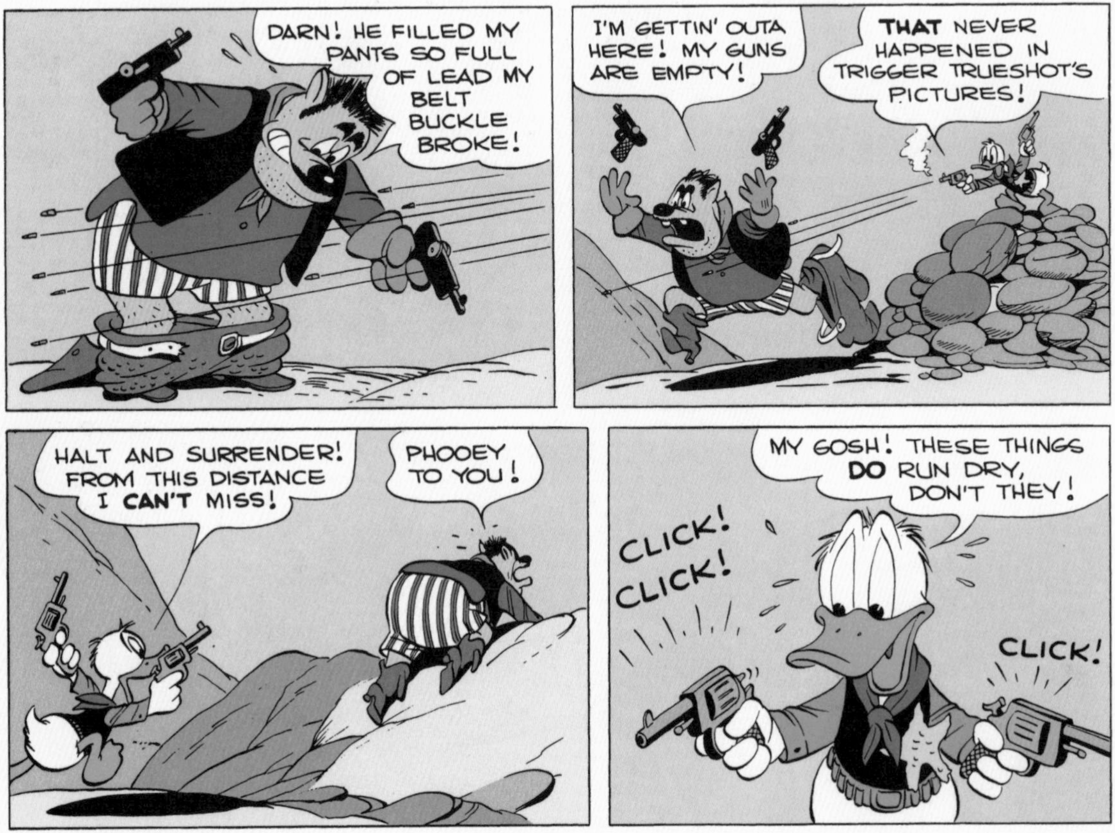
DARN! HE FILLED MY PANTS SO FULL OF LEAD MY BELT BUCKLE BROKE!
I'M GETTIN' OUTA HERE! MY GUNS ARE EMPTY!
THAT NEVER HAPPENED IN TRIGGER TRUESHOT'S PICTURES!
HALT AND SURRENDER! FROM THIS DISTANCE I CAN'T MISS!
PHOOEY TO YOU!
MY GOSH! THESE THINGS DO RUN DRY, DON'T THEY!
CLICK! CLICK!
CLICK!

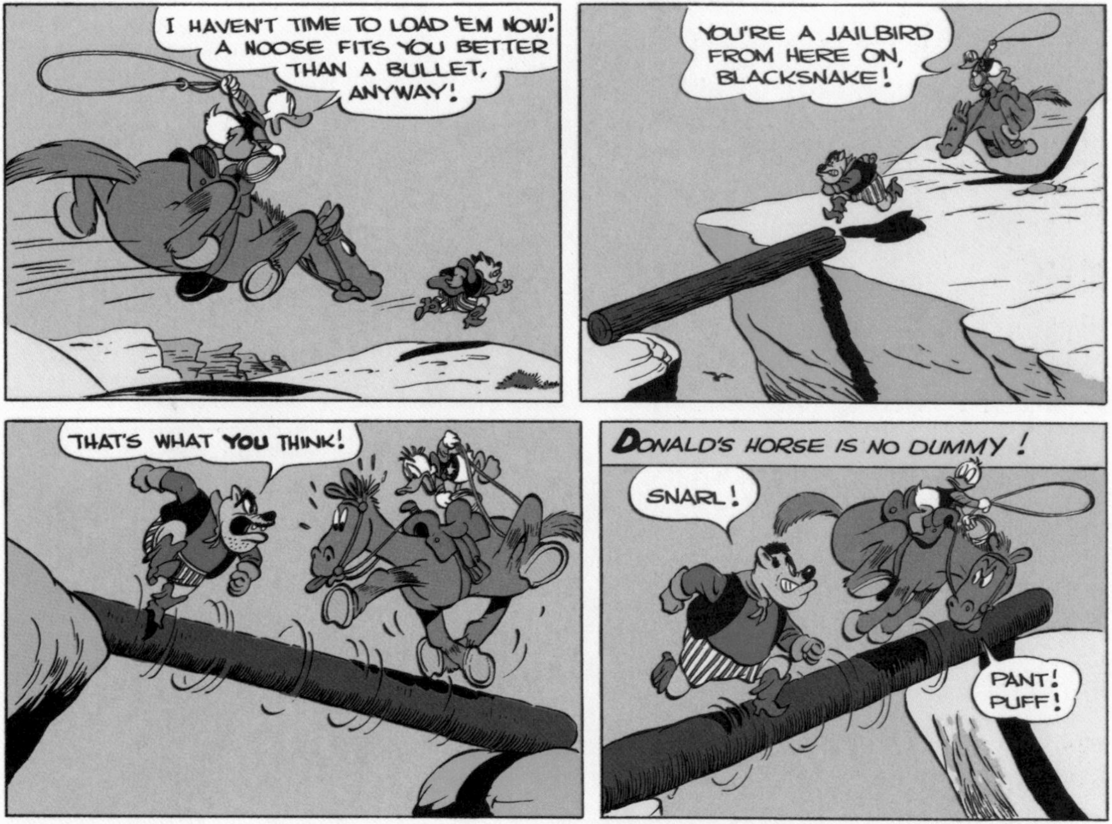
I HAVEN'T TIME TO LOAD 'EM NOW! A NOOSE FITS YOU BETTER THAN A BULLET, ANYWAY!
YOU'RE A JAILBIRD FROM HERE ON, BLACKSNAKE!
THAT'S WHAT **YOU** THINK!
DONALD'S HORSE IS NO DUMMY!
SNARL!
PANT! PUFF!

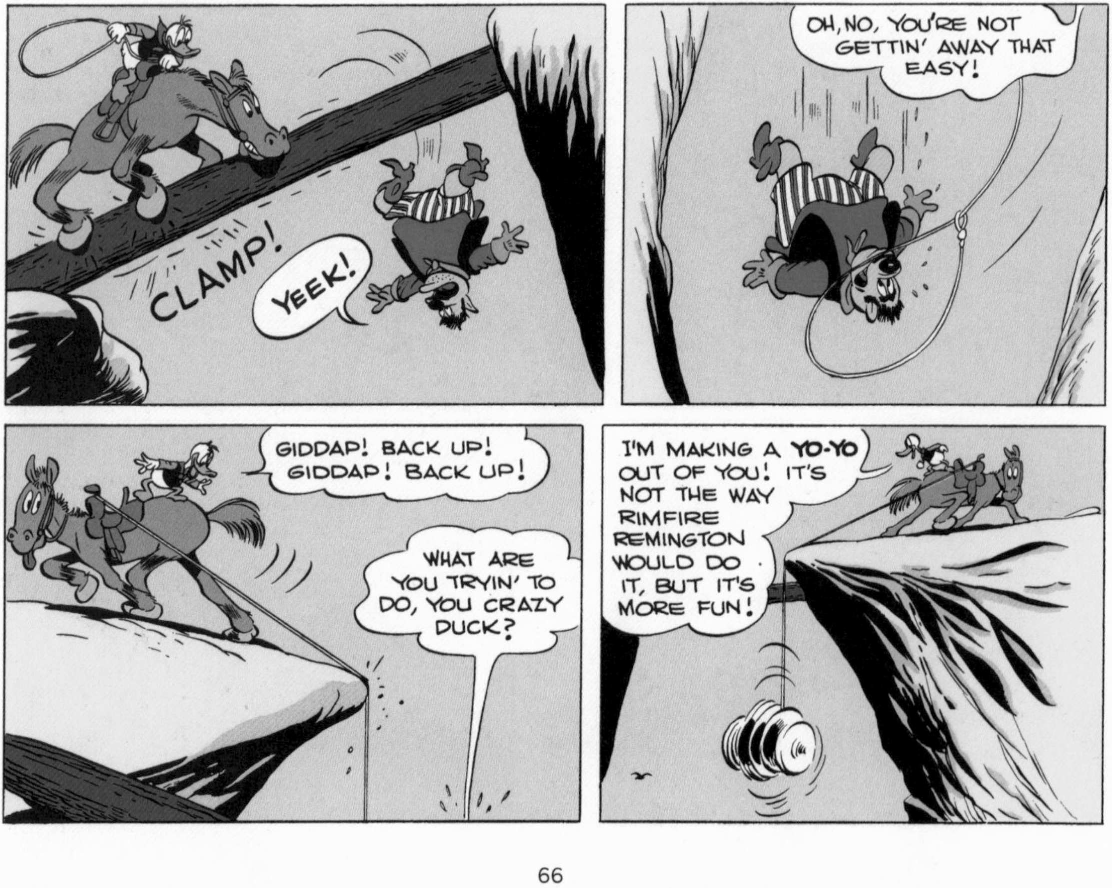
CLAMP!
YEEK!
OH, NO, YOU'RE NOT GETTIN' AWAY THAT EASY!
GIDDAP! BACK UP! GIDDAP! BACK UP!
WHAT ARE YOU TRYIN' TO DO, YOU CRAZY DUCK?
I'M MAKING A YO-YO OUT OF YOU! IT'S NOT THE WAY RIMFIRE REMINGTON WOULD DO IT, BUT IT'S MORE FUN!

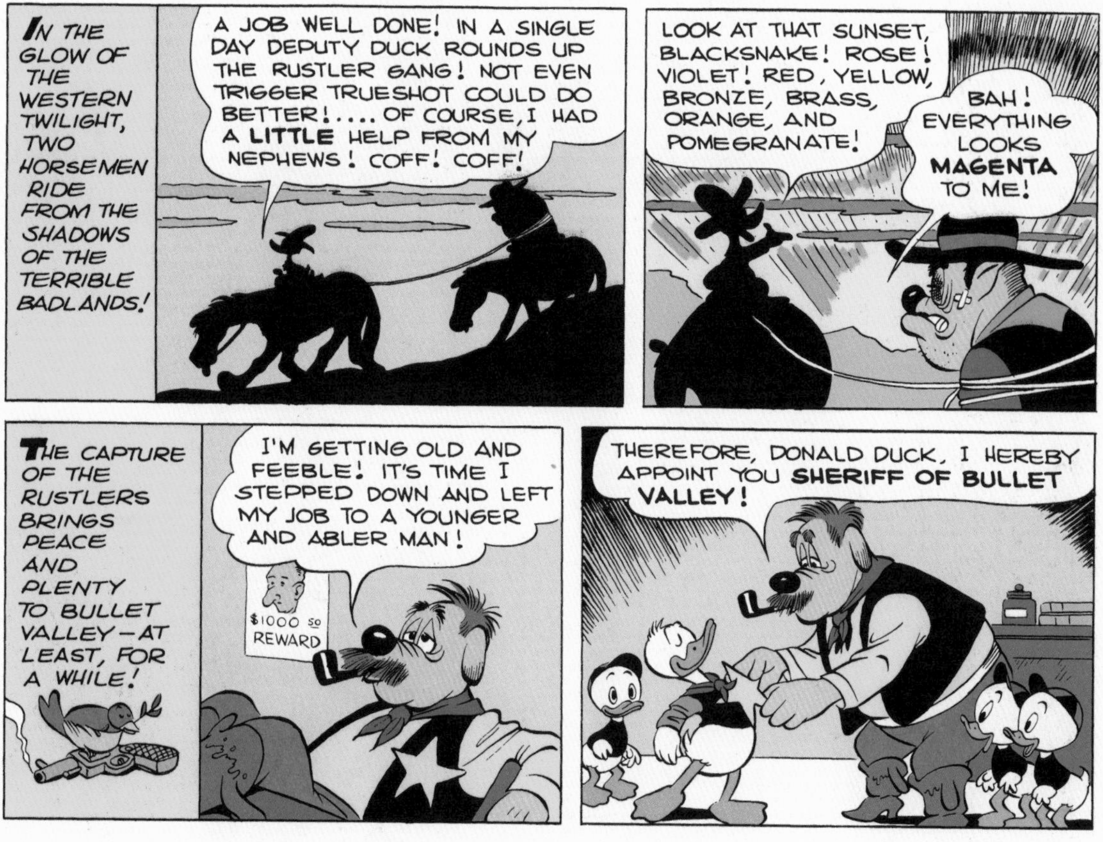
IN THE GLOW OF THE WESTERN TWILIGHT, TWO HORSEMEN RIDE FROM THE SHADOWS OF THE TERRIBLE BADLANDS!
A JOB WELL DONE! IN A SINGLE DAY DEPUTY DUCK ROUNDS UP THE RUSTLER GANG! NOT EVEN TRIGGER TRUESHOT COULD DO BETTER!.... OF COURSE, I HAD A **LITTLE** HELP FROM MY NEPHEWS! COFF! COFF!
LOOK AT THAT SUNSET, BLACKSNAKE! ROSE! VIOLET! RED, YELLOW, BRONZE, BRASS, ORANGE, AND POMEGRANATE!
BAH! EVERYTHING LOOKS **MAGENTA** TO ME!
THE CAPTURE OF THE RUSTLERS BRINGS PEACE AND PLENTY TO BULLET VALLEY—AT LEAST, FOR A WHILE!
I'M GETTING OLD AND FEEBLE! IT'S TIME I STEPPED DOWN AND LEFT MY JOB TO A YOUNGER AND ABLER MAN!
$1000 50
REWARD
THEREFORE, DONALD DUCK, I HEREBY APPOINT YOU **SHERIFF OF BULLET VALLEY**!

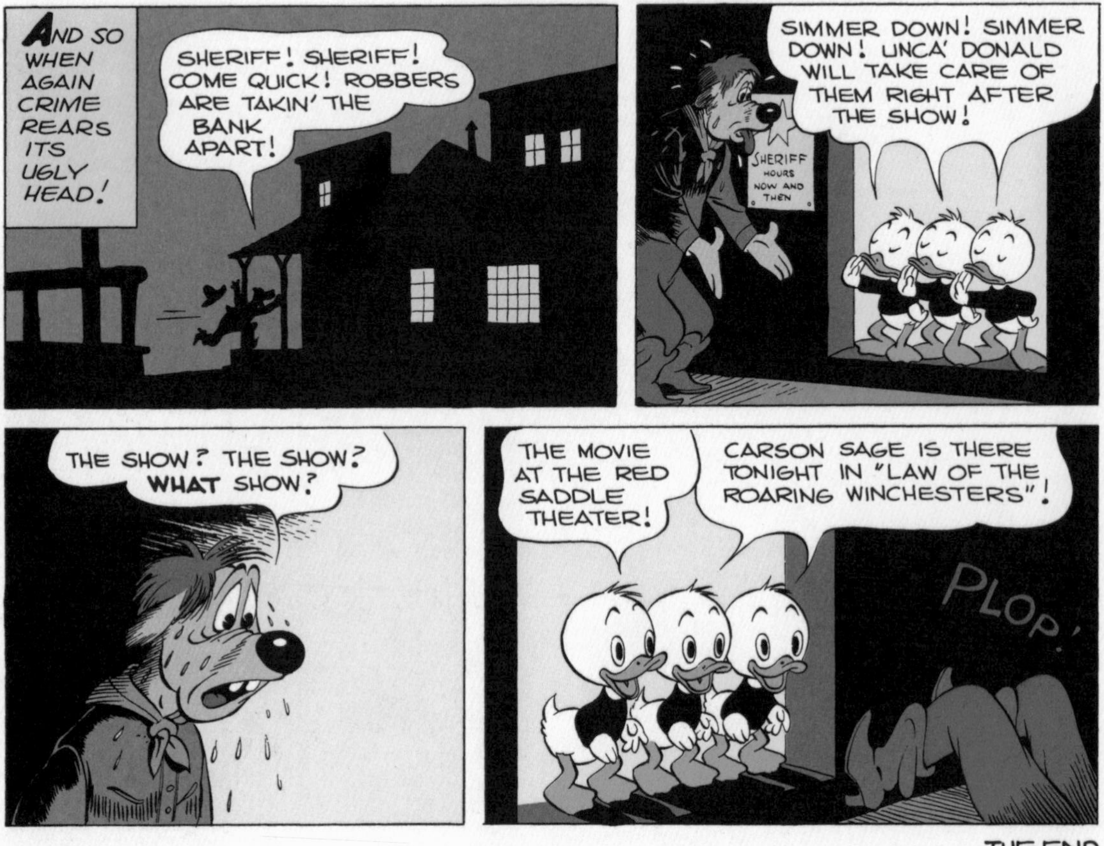
AND SO WHEN AGAIN CRIME REARS ITS UGLY HEAD!
SHERIFF! SHERIFF! COME QUICK! ROBBERS ARE TAKIN' THE BANK APART!
SIMMER DOWN! SIMMER DOWN! UNCA' DONALD WILL TAKE CARE OF THEM RIGHT AFTER THE SHOW!
SHERIFF HOURS NOW AND THEN
THE SHOW? THE SHOW? WHAT SHOW?
THE MOVIE AT THE RED SADDLE THEATER!
CARSON SAGE IS THERE TONIGHT IN "LAW OF THE ROARING WINCHESTERS"!
PLOP!

THE END

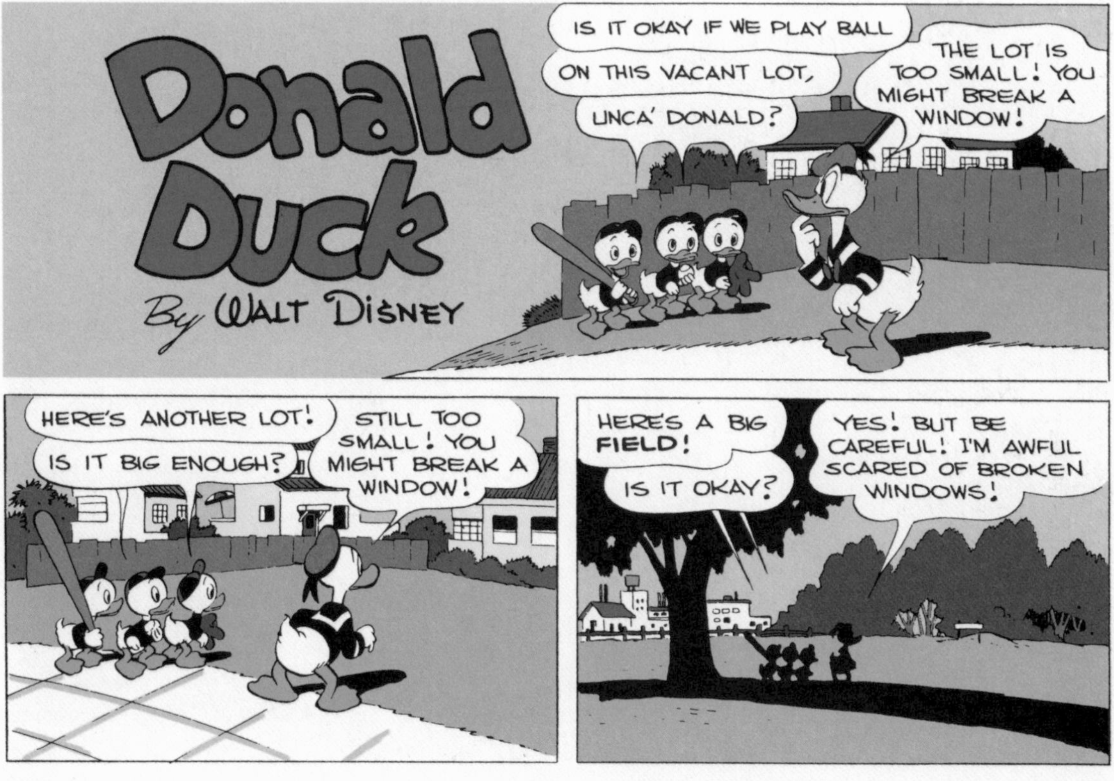
Donald Duck
By Walt Disney
IS IT OKAY IF WE PLAY BALL
ON THIS VACANT LOT,
UNCA' DONALD?
THE LOT IS TOO SMALL! YOU MIGHT BREAK A WINDOW!
HERE'S ANOTHER LOT!
IS IT BIG ENOUGH?
STILL TOO SMALL! YOU MIGHT BREAK A WINDOW!
HERE'S A BIG **FIELD**!
IS IT OKAY?
YES! BUT BE CAREFUL! I'M AWFUL SCARED OF BROKEN WINDOWS!

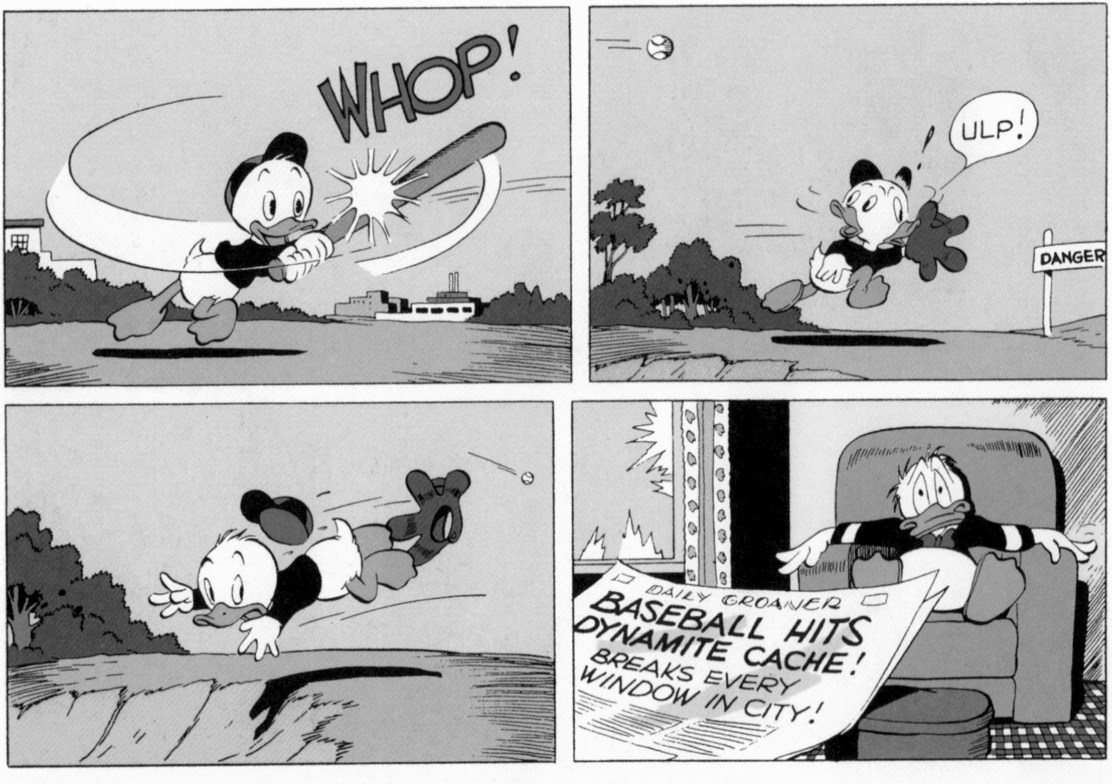
WHOP!
ULP!
DANGER
DAILY GROANER
BASEBALL HITS DYNAMITE CACHE!
BREAKS EVERY WINDOW IN CITY!

THE END

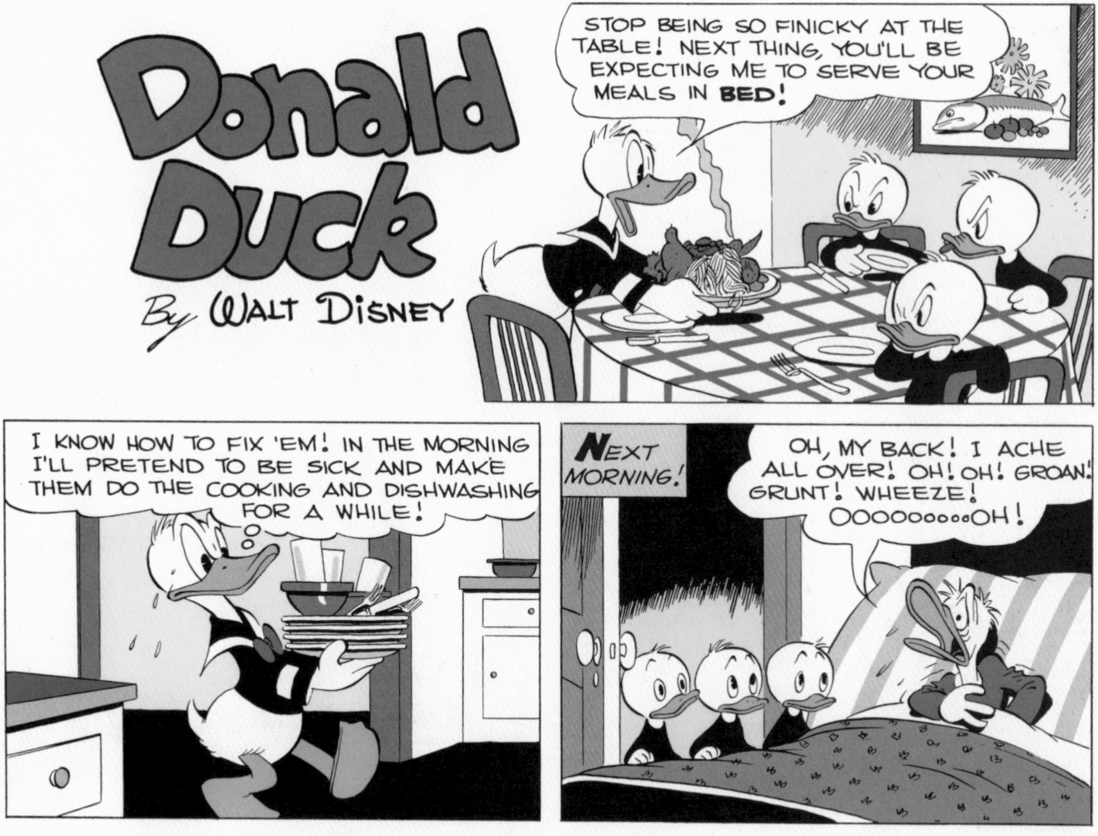
Donald Duck
By Walt Disney
STOP BEING SO FINICKY AT THE TABLE! NEXT THING, YOU'LL BE EXPECTING ME TO SERVE YOUR MEALS IN **BED**!
I KNOW HOW TO FIX 'EM! IN THE MORNING I'LL PRETEND TO BE SICK AND MAKE THEM DO THE COOKING AND DISHWASHING FOR A WHILE!
NEXT MORNING!
OH, MY BACK! I ACHE ALL OVER! OH! OH! GROAN! GRUNT! WHEEZE! OOOOOOOOOOH!

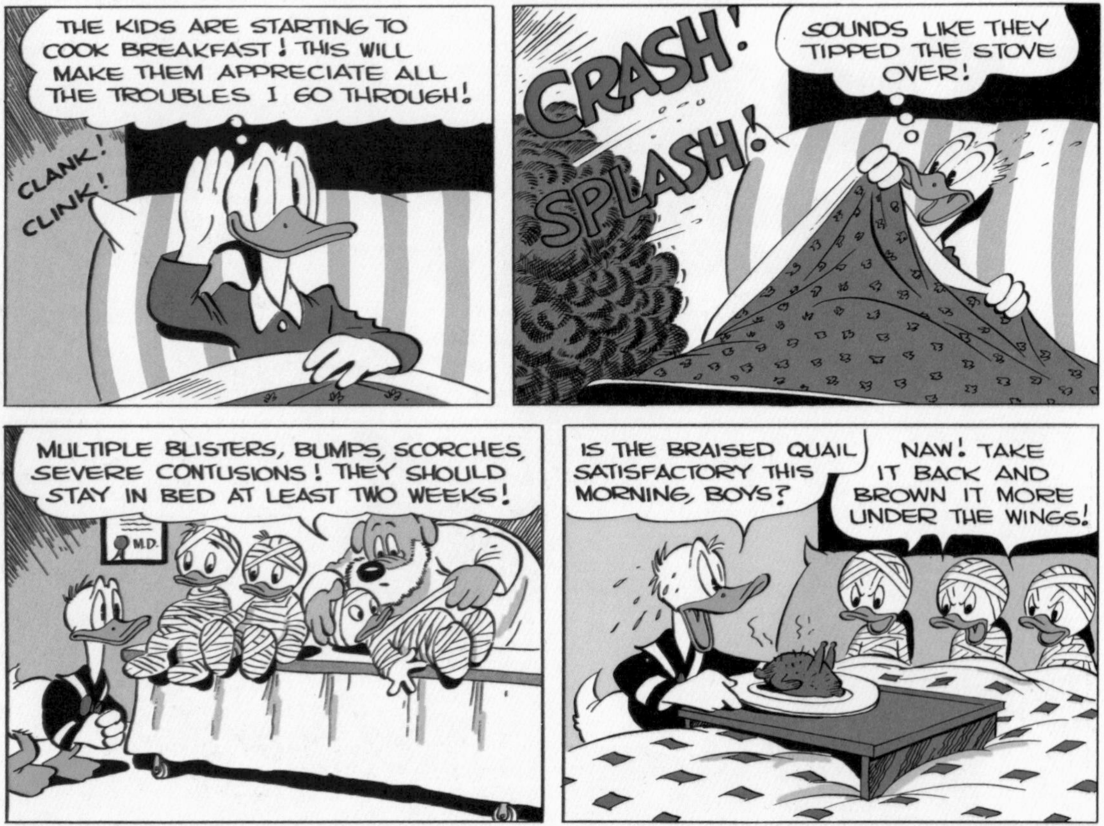
THE KIDS ARE STARTING TO COOK BREAKFAST! THIS WILL MAKE THEM APPRECIATE ALL THE TROUBLES I GO THROUGH!
CLANK! CLINK!
CRASH!
SPLASH!
SOUNDS LIKE THEY TIPPED THE STOVE OVER!
MULTIPLE BLISTERS, BUMPS, SCORCHES, SEVERE CONTUSIONS! THEY SHOULD STAY IN BED AT LEAST TWO WEEKS!
M.D.
IS THE BRAISED QUAIL SATISFACTORY THIS MORNING, BOYS?
NAW! TAKE IT BACK AND BROWN IT MORE UNDER THE WINGS!

THE END

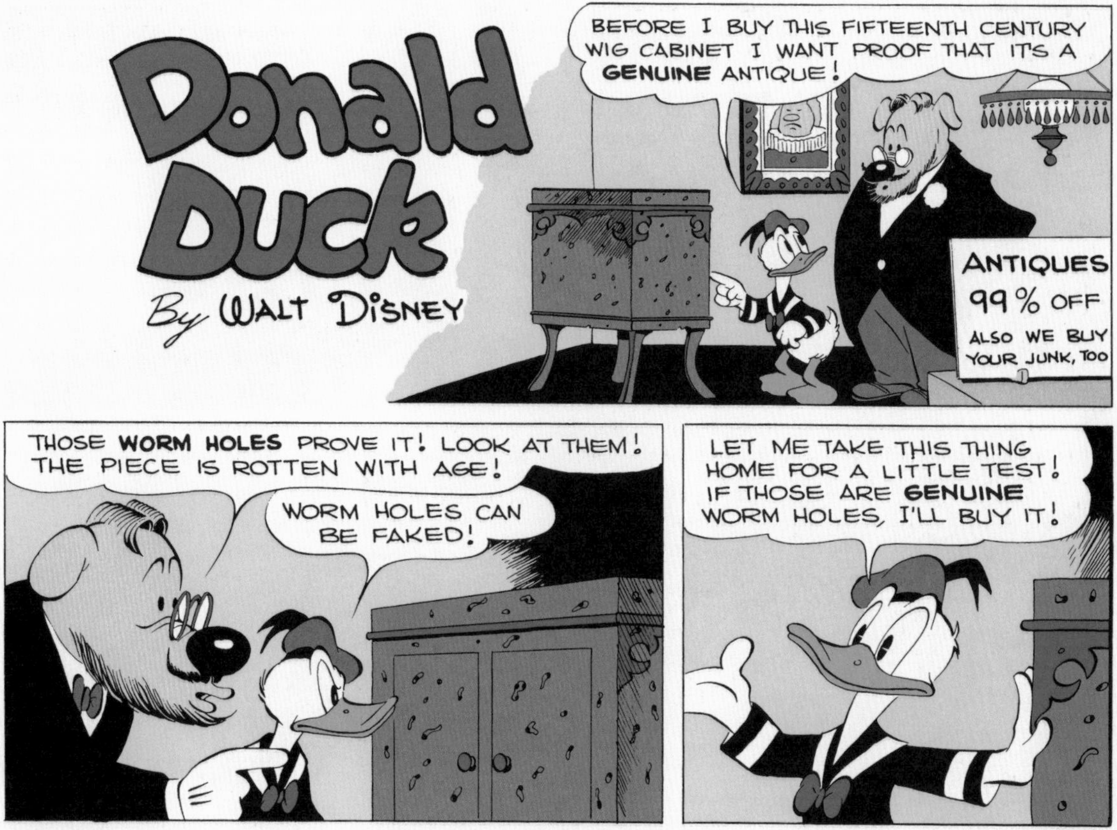
Donald Duck
By Walt Disney
BEFORE I BUY THIS FIFTEENTH CENTURY WIG CABINET I WANT PROOF THAT IT'S A **GENUINE** ANTIQUE!
ANTIQUES 99% OFF ALSO WE BUY YOUR JUNK, TOO
THOSE **WORM HOLES** PROVE IT! LOOK AT THEM! THE PIECE IS ROTTEN WITH AGE!
WORM HOLES CAN BE FAKED!
LET ME TAKE THIS THING HOME FOR A LITTLE TEST! IF THOSE ARE **GENUINE** WORM HOLES, I'LL BUY IT!

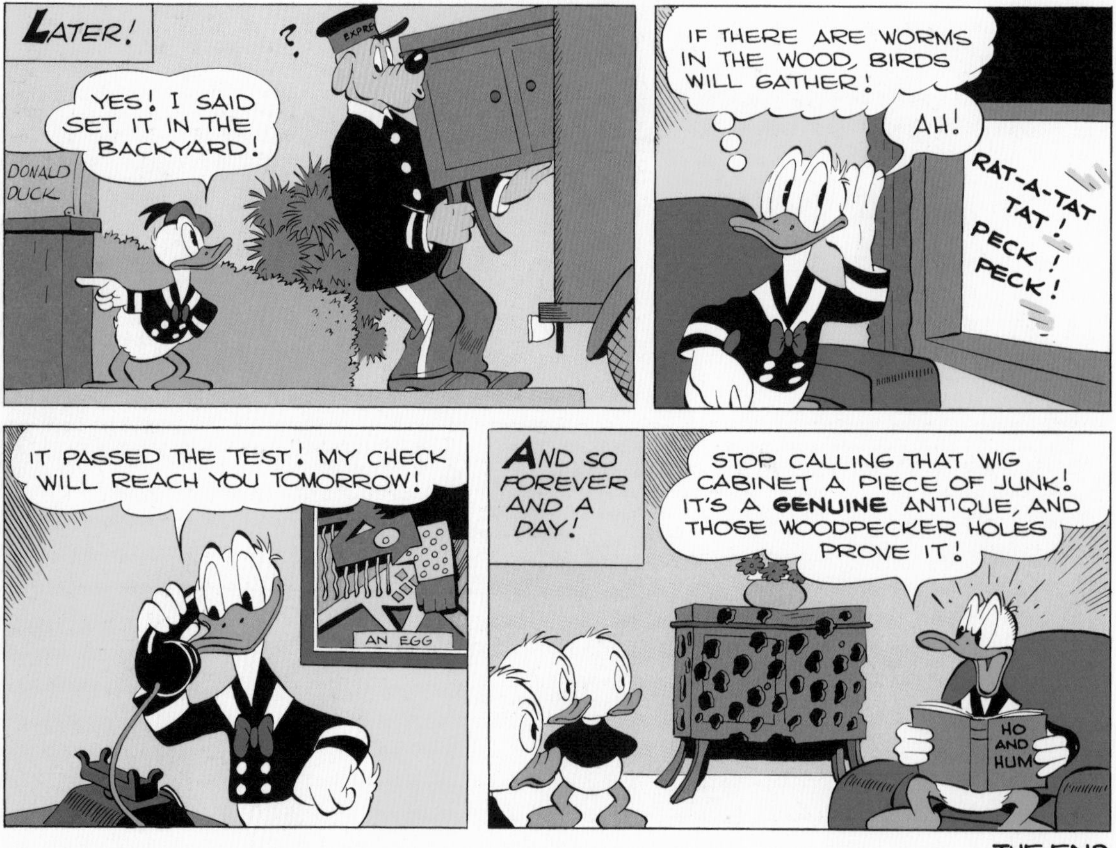
LATER!
YES! I SAID SET IT IN THE BACKYARD!
DONALD DUCK
IF THERE ARE WORMS IN THE WOOD, BIRDS WILL GATHER!
AH!
RAT-A-TAT TAT! PECK! PECK!
IT PASSED THE TEST! MY CHECK WILL REACH YOU TOMORROW!
AN EGG
AND SO FOREVER AND A DAY!
STOP CALLING THAT WIG CABINET A PIECE OF JUNK! IT'S A GENUINE ANTIQUE, AND THOSE WOODPECKER HOLES PROVE IT!
HO AND HUM

THE END

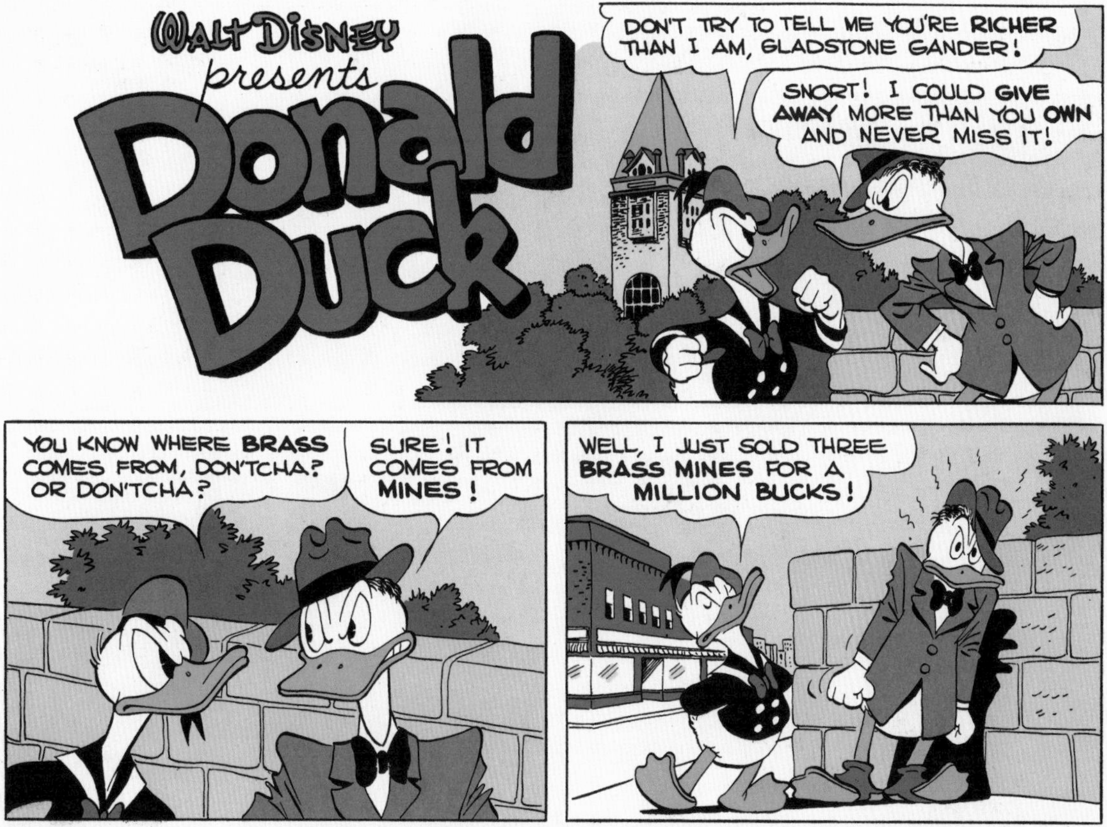
WALT DISNEY
presents
Donald Duck
DON'T TRY TO TELL ME YOU'RE RICHER THAN I AM, GLADSTONE GANDER!
SNORT! I COULD GIVE AWAY MORE THAN YOU OWN AND NEVER MISS IT!
YOU KNOW WHERE BRASS COMES FROM, DON'TCHA? OR DON'TCHA?
SURE! IT COMES FROM MINES!
WELL, I JUST SOLD THREE BRASS MINES FOR A MILLION BUCKS!

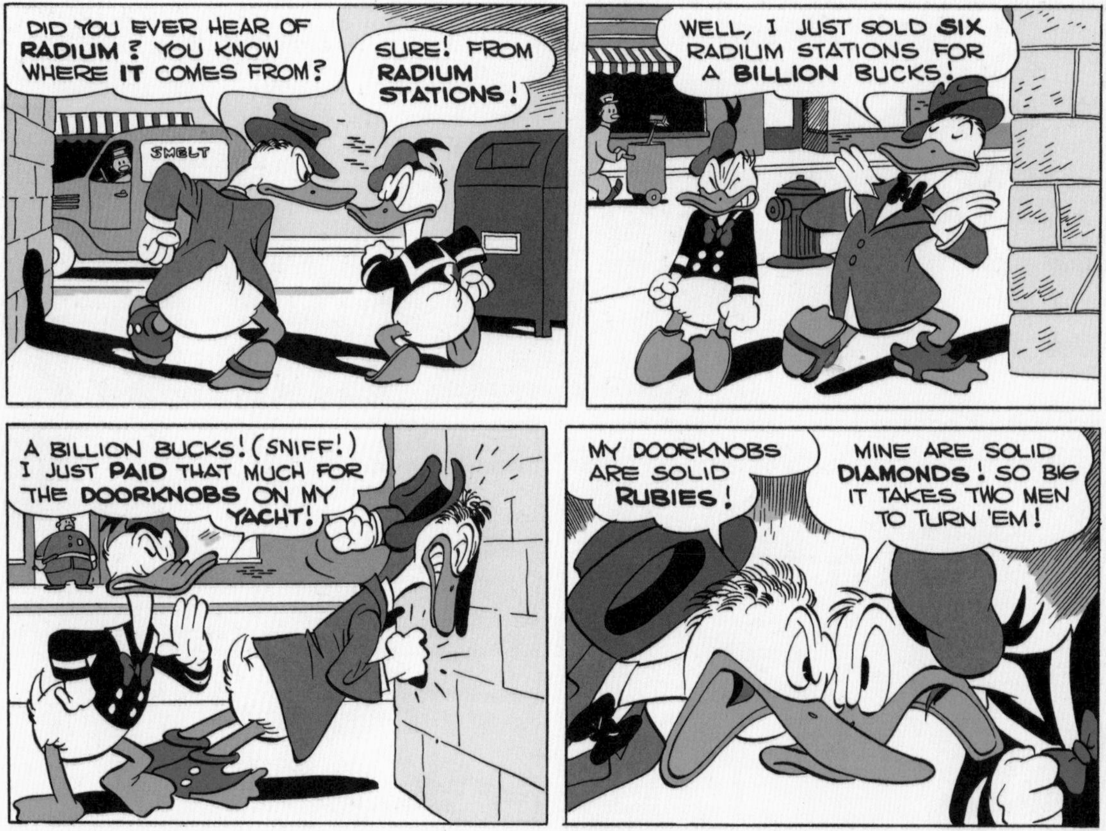
DID YOU EVER HEAR OF RADIUM ? YOU KNOW WHERE IT COMES FROM?
SMELT
SURE! FROM RADIUM STATIONS!
WELL, I JUST SOLD SIX RADIUM STATIONS FOR A BILLION BUCKS!
A BILLION BUCKS! (SNIFF!) I JUST PAID THAT MUCH FOR THE DOORKNOBS ON MY YACHT!
MY DOORKNOBS ARE SOLID RUBIES!
MINE ARE SOLID DIAMONDS! SO BIG IT TAKES TWO MEN TO TURN 'EM!

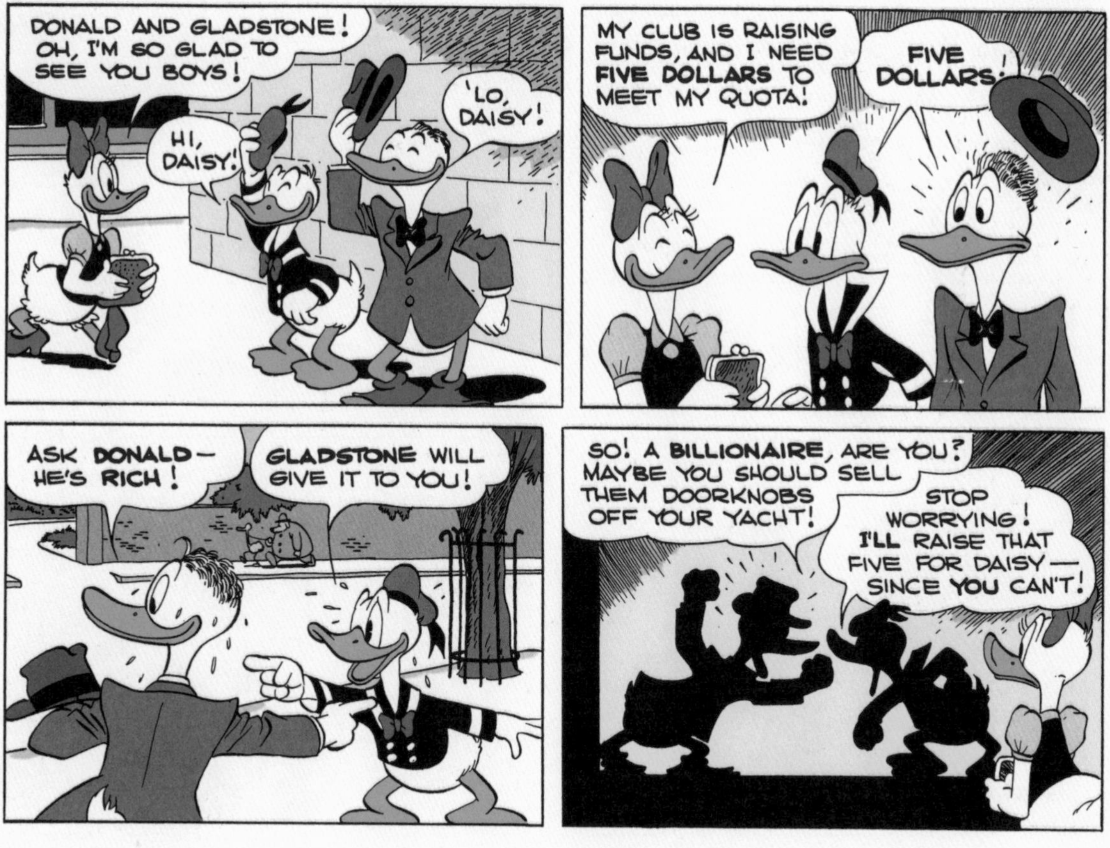
DONALD AND GLADSTONE! OH, I'M SO GLAD TO SEE YOU BOYS!
HI, DAISY!
'LO, DAISY!
MY CLUB IS RAISING FUNDS, AND I NEED **FIVE DOLLARS** TO MEET MY QUOTA!
FIVE DOLLARS!
ASK **DONALD**— HE'S **RICH**!
GLADSTONE WILL GIVE IT TO YOU!
SO! A **BILLIONAIRE**, ARE YOU? MAYBE YOU SHOULD SELL THEM DOORKNOBS OFF YOUR YACHT!
STOP WORRYING! **I'LL** RAISE THAT FIVE FOR DAISY— SINCE **YOU** CAN'T!

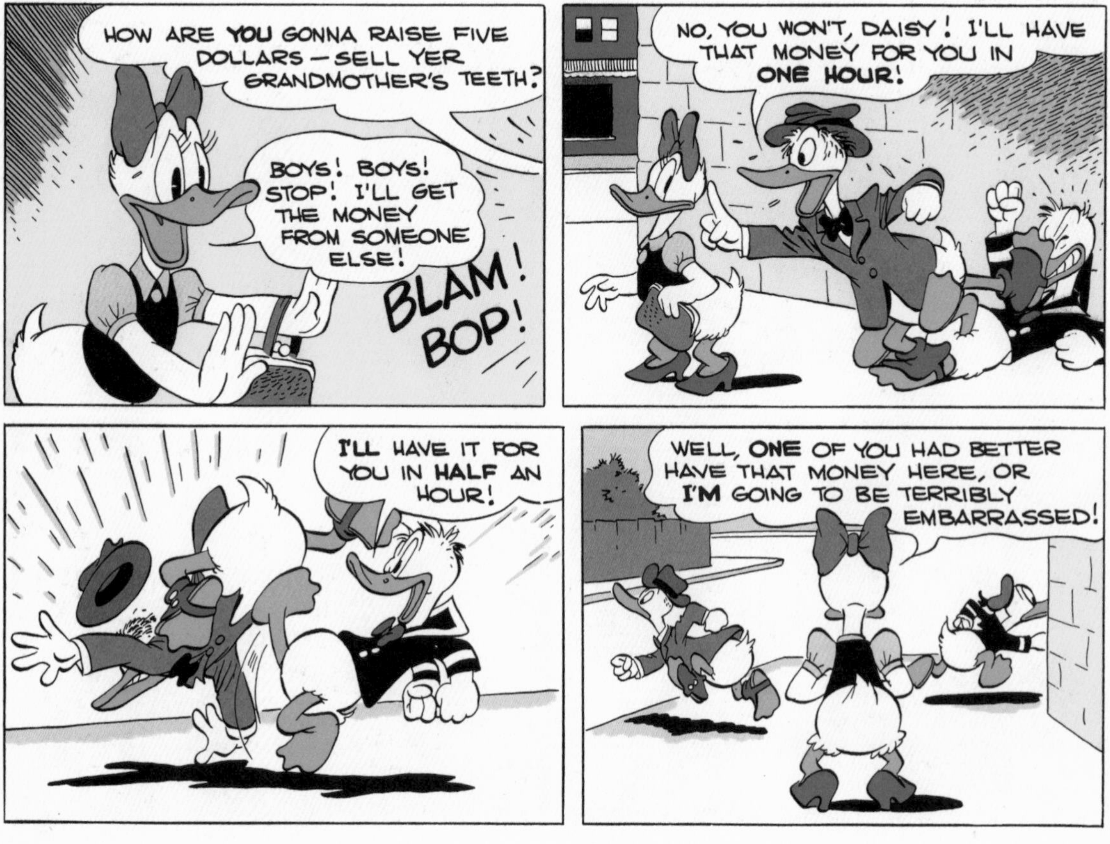
HOW ARE **YOU** GONNA RAISE FIVE DOLLARS — SELL YER GRANDMOTHER'S TEETH?
BOYS! BOYS! STOP! I'LL GET THE MONEY FROM SOMEONE ELSE!
BLAM! BOP!
NO, YOU WON'T, DAISY! I'LL HAVE THAT MONEY FOR YOU IN **ONE HOUR**!
I'LL HAVE IT FOR YOU IN **HALF** AN HOUR!
WELL, **ONE** OF YOU HAD BETTER HAVE THAT MONEY HERE, OR **I'M** GOING TO BE TERRIBLY EMBARRASSED!

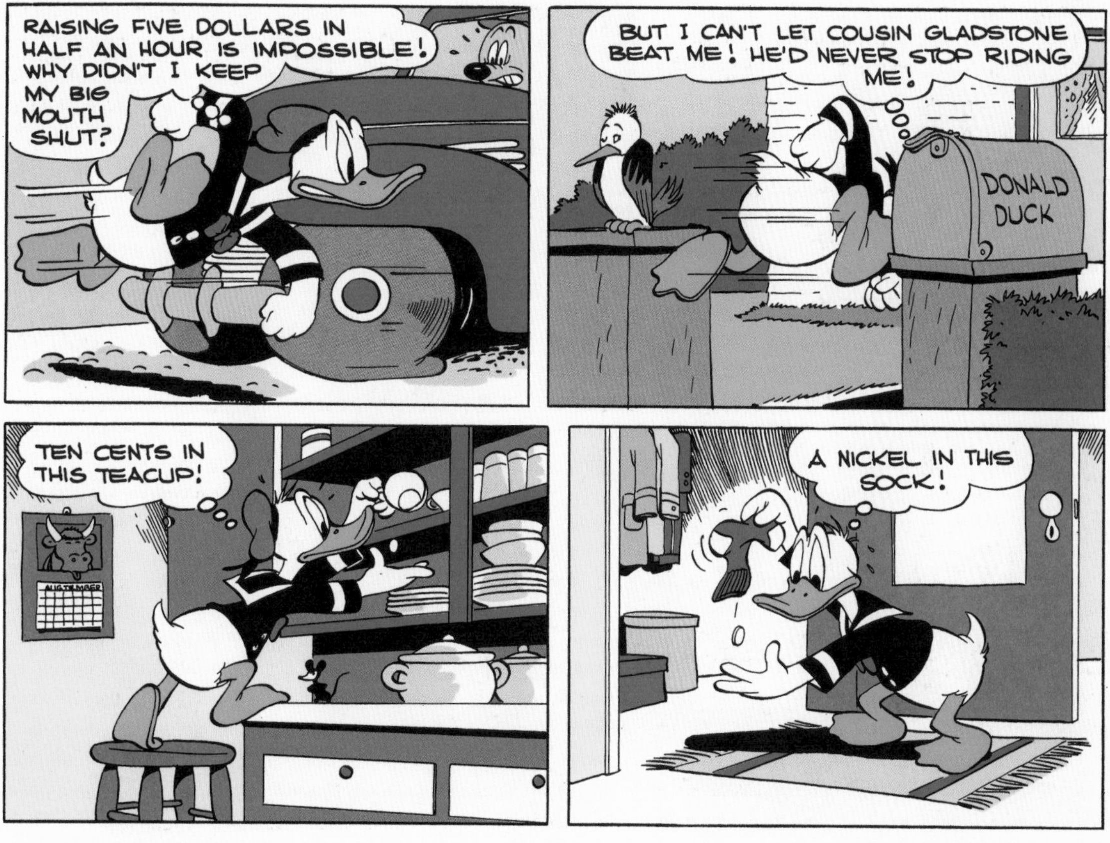
RAISING FIVE DOLLARS IN HALF AN HOUR IS IMPOSSIBLE! WHY DIDN'T I KEEP MY BIG MOUTH SHUT?
BUT I CAN'T LET COUSIN GLADSTONE BEAT ME! HE'D NEVER STOP RIDING ME!
DONALD DUCK
TEN CENTS IN THIS TEACUP!
A NICKEL IN THIS SOCK!

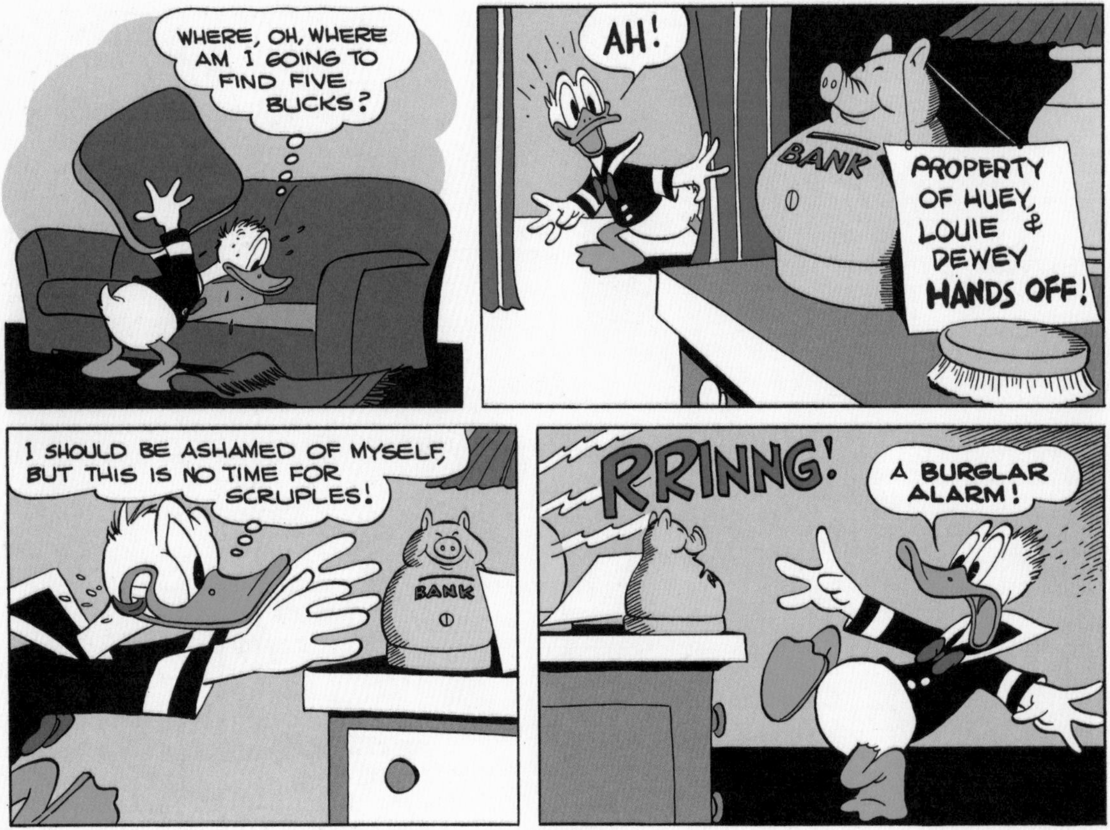
WHERE, OH, WHERE AM I GOING TO FIND FIVE BUCKS?
AH!
BANK
PROPERTY OF HUEY, LOUIE & DEWEY HANDS OFF!
I SHOULD BE ASHAMED OF MYSELF, BUT THIS IS NO TIME FOR SCRUPLES!
BANK
RRINNG!
A BURGLAR ALARM!

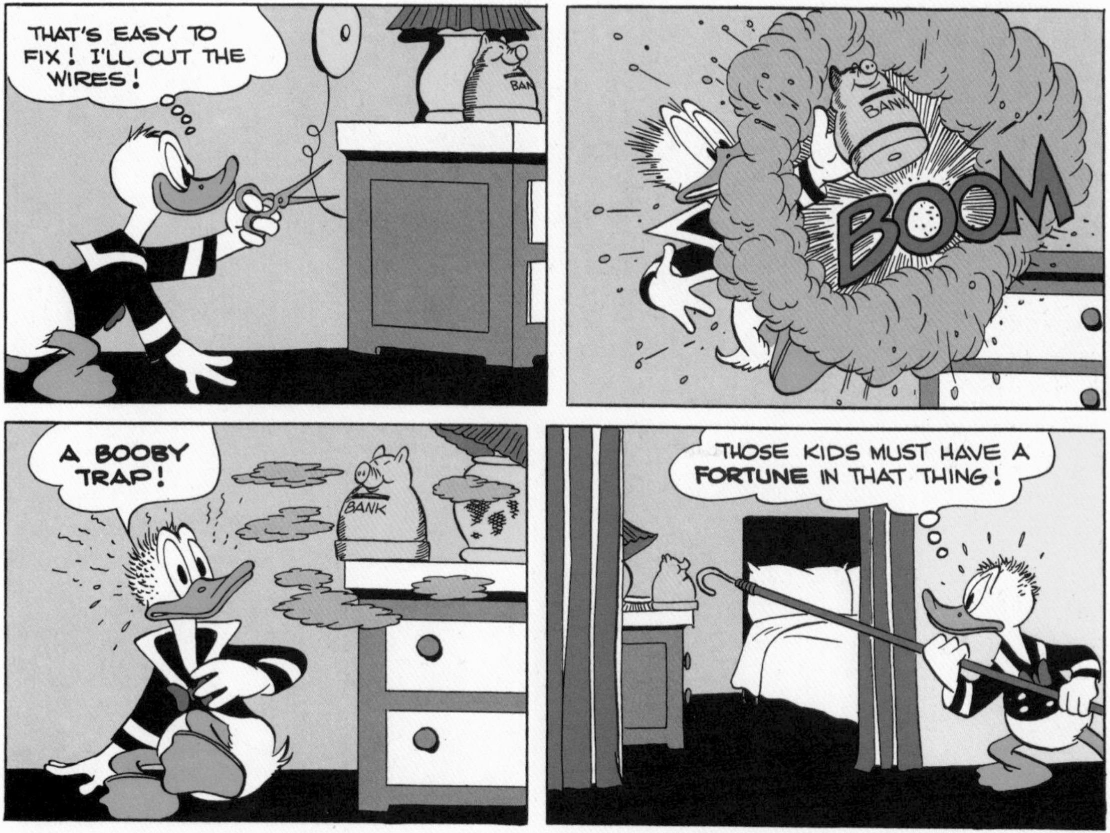
THAT'S EASY TO FIX! I'LL CUT THE WIRES!
BANK
BANK
BOOM
A BOOBY TRAP!
BANK
THOSE KIDS MUST HAVE A FORTUNE IN THAT THING!

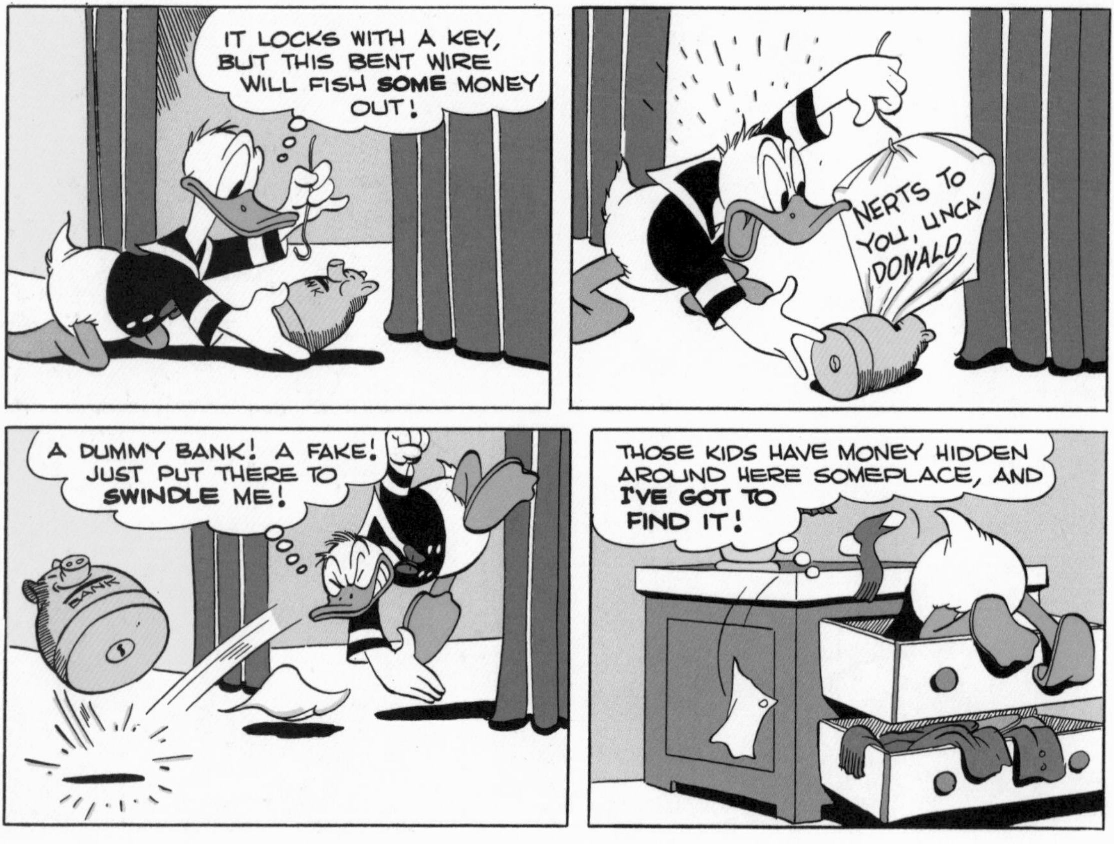
IT LOCKS WITH A KEY, BUT THIS BENT WIRE WILL FISH **SOME** MONEY OUT!
NERTS TO YOU, UNCA' DONALD
A DUMMY BANK! A FAKE! JUST PUT THERE TO **SWINDLE** ME!
BANK
THOSE KIDS HAVE MONEY HIDDEN AROUND HERE SOMEPLACE, AND **I'VE GOT TO FIND IT!**

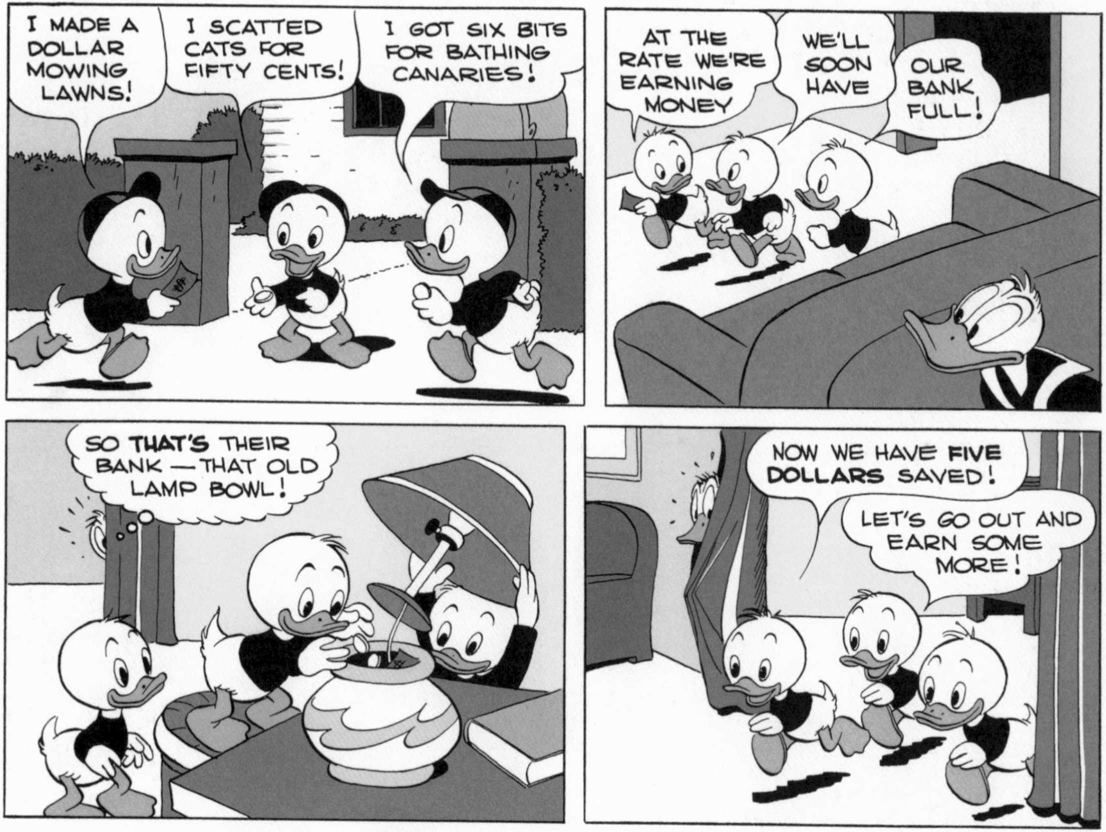

I MADE A DOLLAR MOWING LAWNS!
I SCATTED CATS FOR FIFTY CENTS!
I GOT SIX BITS FOR BATHING CANARIES!
AT THE RATE WE'RE EARNING MONEY
WE'LL SOON HAVE
OUR BANK FULL!
SO **THAT'S** THEIR BANK — THAT OLD LAMP BOWL!
NOW WE HAVE **FIVE DOLLARS** SAVED!
LET'S GO OUT AND EARN SOME MORE!

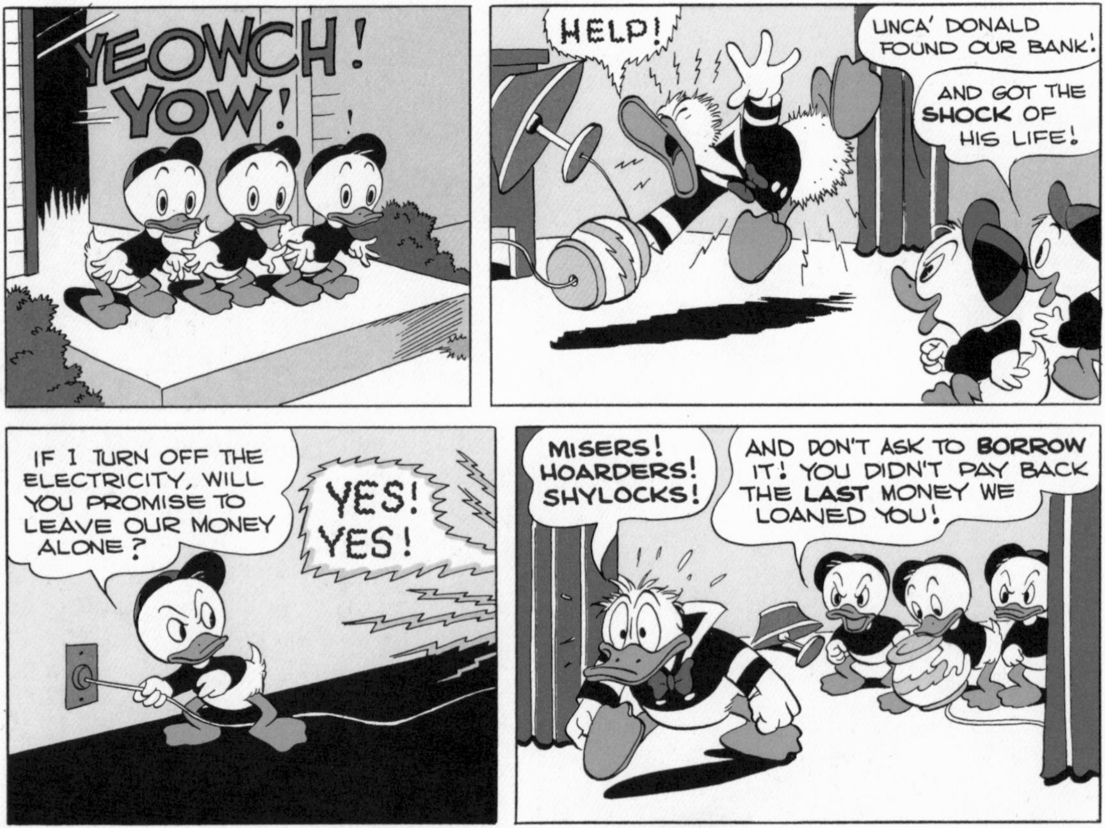
YEOWCH! YOW!
!
HELP!
UNCA' DONALD FOUND OUR BANK!
AND GOT THE **SHOCK** OF HIS LIFE!
IF I TURN OFF THE ELECTRICITY, WILL YOU PROMISE TO LEAVE OUR MONEY ALONE?
YES! YES!
MISERS! HOARDERS! SHYLOCKS!
AND DON'T ASK TO **BORROW** IT! YOU DIDN'T PAY BACK THE **LAST** MONEY WE LOANED YOU!

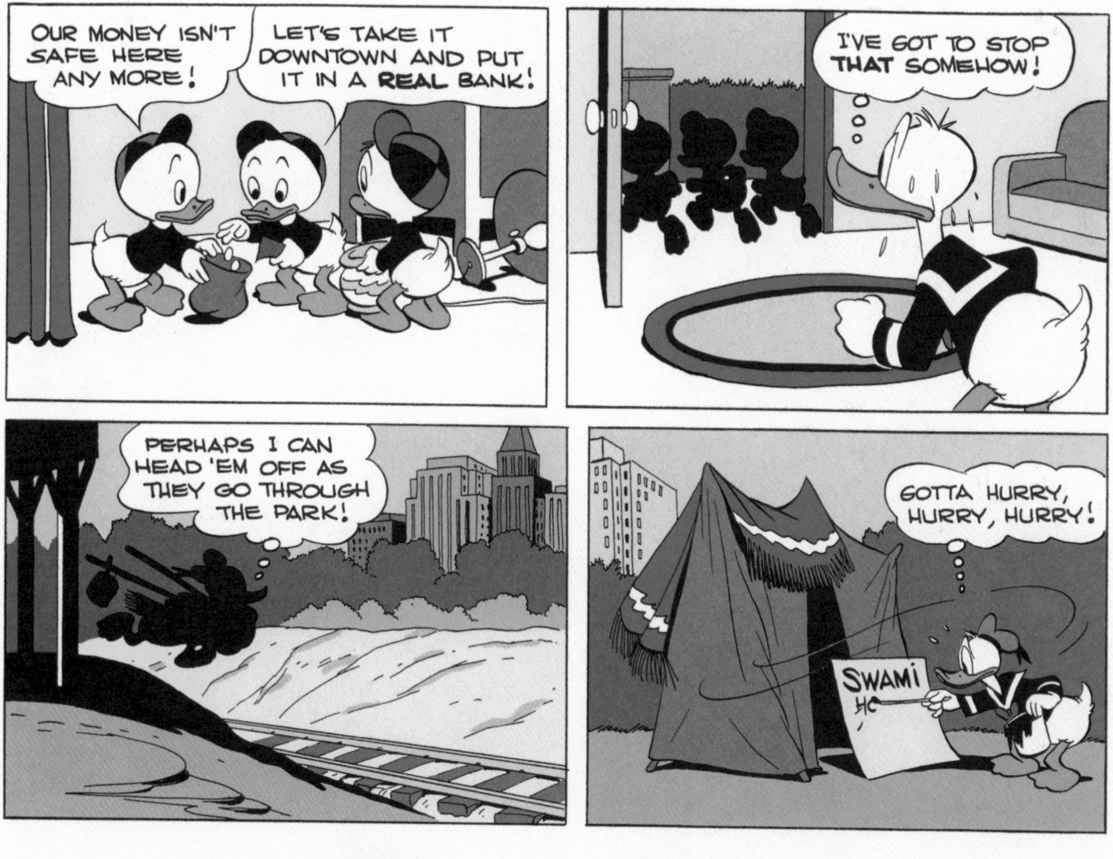
OUR MONEY ISN'T SAFE HERE ANY MORE!
LET'S TAKE IT DOWNTOWN AND PUT IT IN A **REAL** BANK!
I'VE GOT TO STOP **THAT** SOMEHOW!
PERHAPS I CAN HEAD 'EM OFF AS THEY GO THROUGH THE PARK!
GOTTA HURRY, HURRY, HURRY!
SWAMI

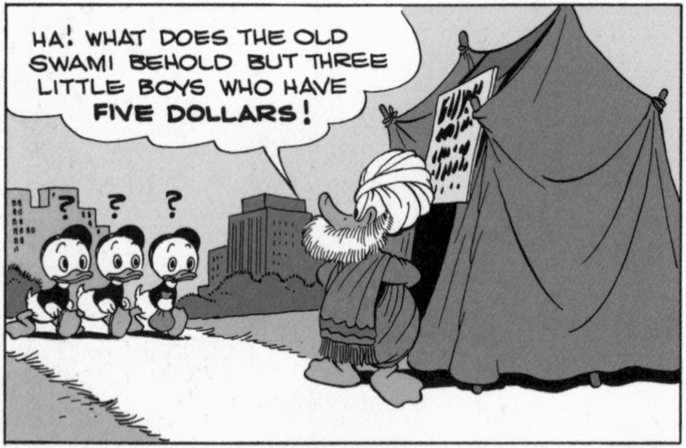
HA! WHAT DOES THE OLD SWAMI BEHOLD BUT THREE LITTLE BOYS WHO HAVE **FIVE DOLLARS**!
?
?
?

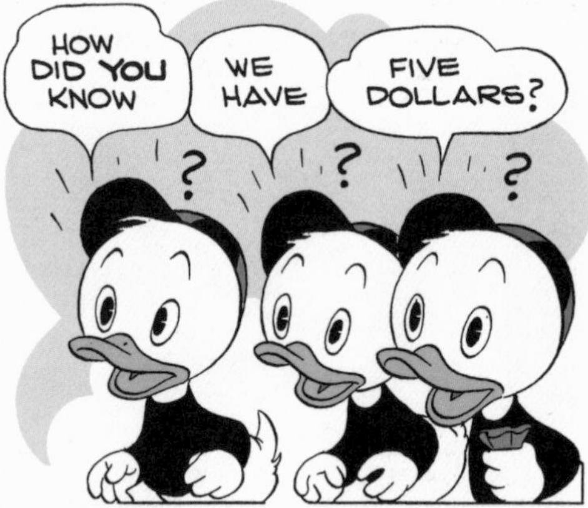
HOW DID **YOU** KNOW
WE HAVE
FIVE DOLLARS?
?
?
?

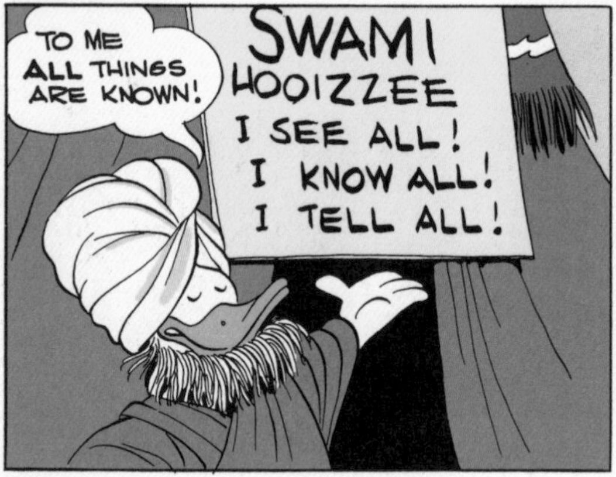
TO ME **ALL** THINGS ARE KNOWN!
SWAMI HOOIZZEE
I SEE ALL!
I KNOW ALL!
I TELL ALL!

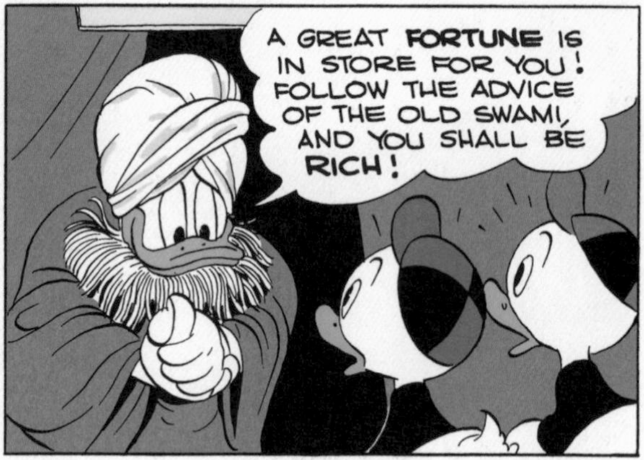
A GREAT **FORTUNE** IS IN STORE FOR YOU! FOLLOW THE ADVICE OF THE OLD SWAMI, AND YOU SHALL BE **RICH**!

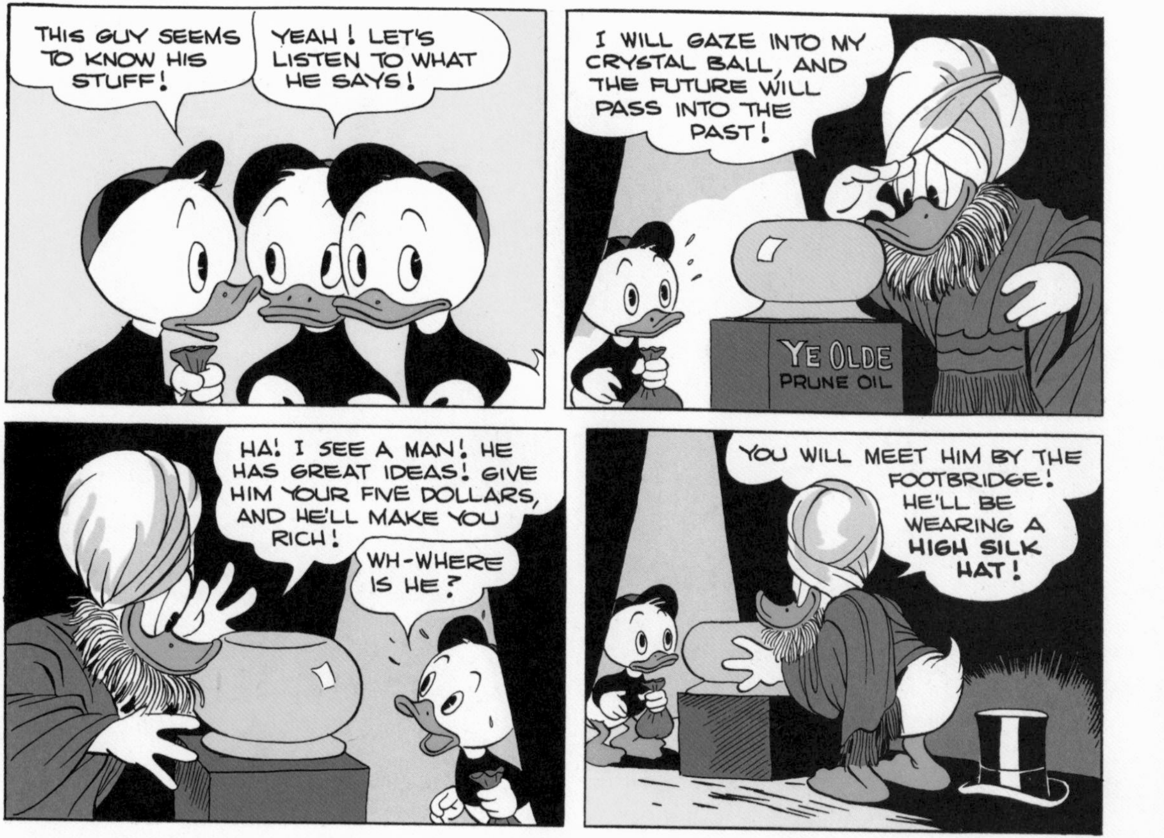
THIS GUY SEEMS TO KNOW HIS STUFF!
YEAH! LET'S LISTEN TO WHAT HE SAYS!
I WILL GAZE INTO MY CRYSTAL BALL, AND THE FUTURE WILL PASS INTO THE PAST!
YE OLDE PRUNE OIL
HA! I SEE A MAN! HE HAS GREAT IDEAS! GIVE HIM YOUR FIVE DOLLARS, AND HE'LL MAKE YOU RICH!
WH-WHERE IS HE?
YOU WILL MEET HIM BY THE FOOTBRIDGE! HE'LL BE WEARING A **HIGH SILK HAT**!

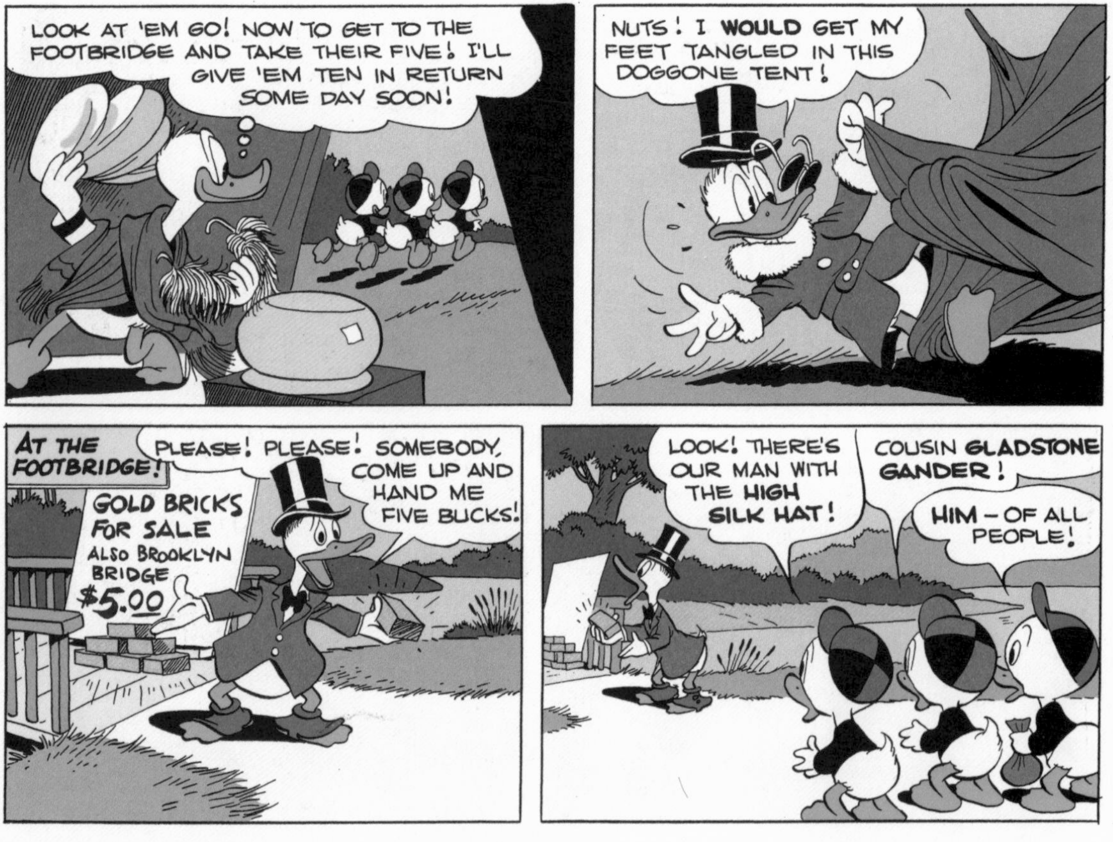
LOOK AT 'EM GO! NOW TO GET TO THE FOOTBRIDGE AND TAKE THEIR FIVE! I'LL GIVE 'EM TEN IN RETURN SOME DAY SOON!
NUTS! I **WOULD** GET MY FEET TANGLED IN THIS DOGGONE TENT!
AT THE FOOTBRIDGE!
PLEASE! PLEASE! SOMEBODY, COME UP AND HAND ME FIVE BUCKS!
GOLD BRICKS FOR SALE ALSO BROOKLYN BRIDGE $5.00
LOOK! THERE'S OUR MAN WITH THE **HIGH SILK HAT**!
COUSIN **GLADSTONE GANDER**!
HIM – OF ALL PEOPLE!

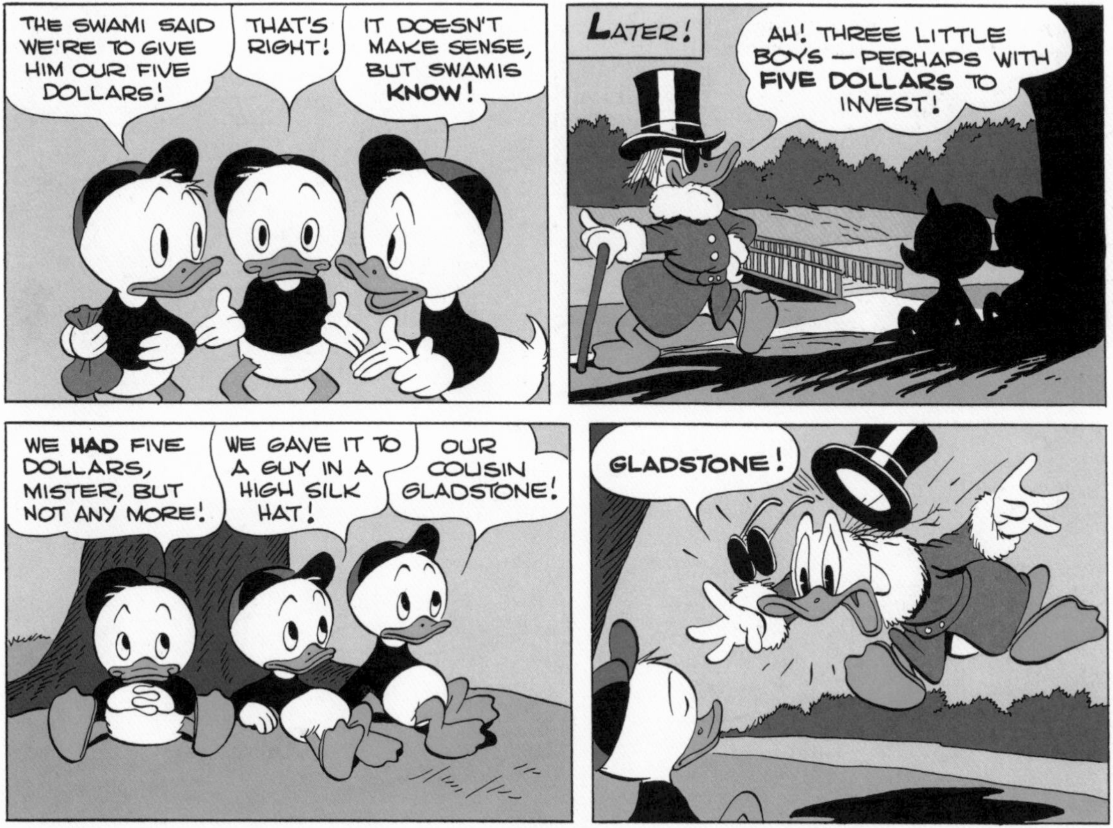
THE SWAMI SAID WE'RE TO GIVE HIM OUR FIVE DOLLARS!
THAT'S RIGHT!
IT DOESN'T MAKE SENSE, BUT SWAMIS **KNOW**!
LATER!
AH! THREE LITTLE BOYS — PERHAPS WITH **FIVE DOLLARS** TO INVEST!
WE **HAD** FIVE DOLLARS, MISTER, BUT NOT ANY MORE!
WE GAVE IT TO A GUY IN A HIGH SILK HAT!
OUR COUSIN GLADSTONE!
GLADSTONE!

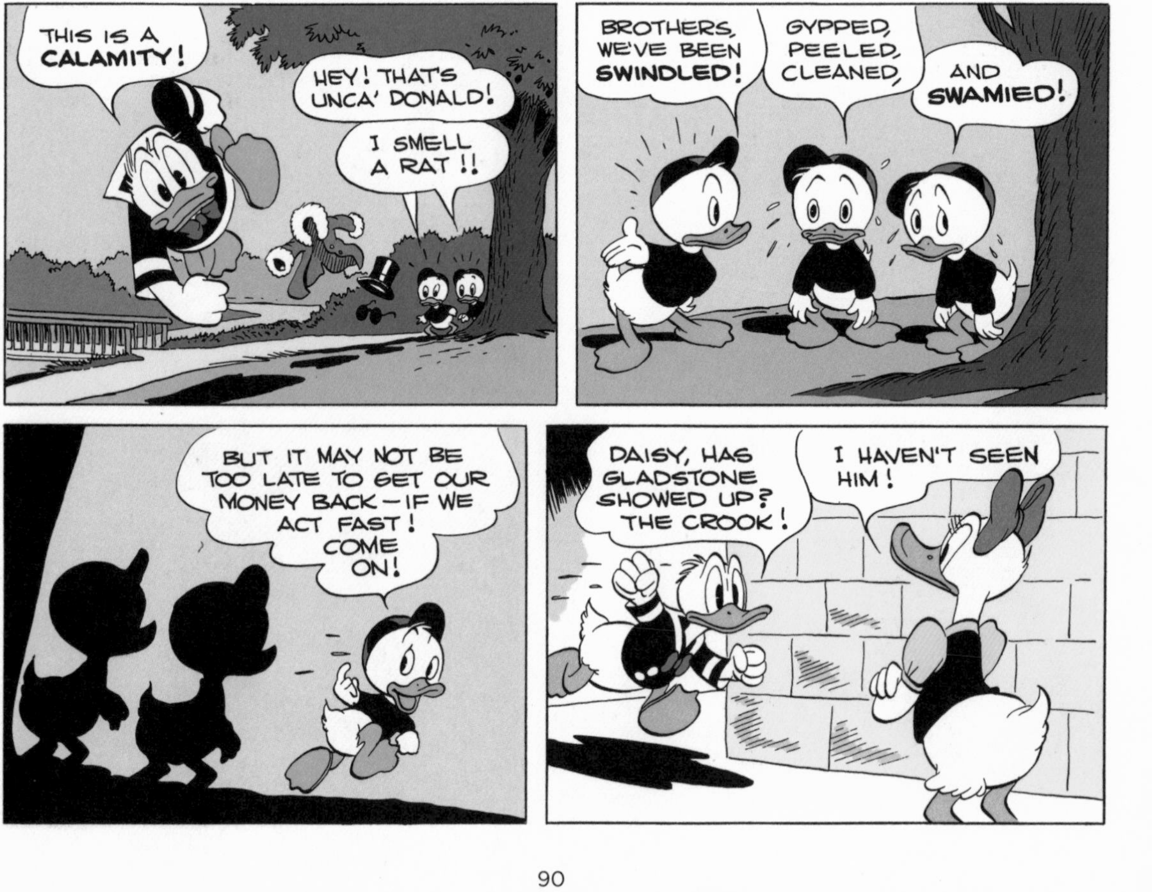
THIS IS A CALAMITY!
HEY! THAT'S UNCA' DONALD!
I SMELL A RAT!!
BROTHERS, WE'VE BEEN SWINDLED!
GYPPED, PEELED, CLEANED,
AND SWAMIED!
BUT IT MAY NOT BE TOO LATE TO GET OUR MONEY BACK—IF WE ACT FAST! COME ON!
DAISY, HAS GLADSTONE SHOWED UP? THE CROOK!
I HAVEN'T SEEN HIM!

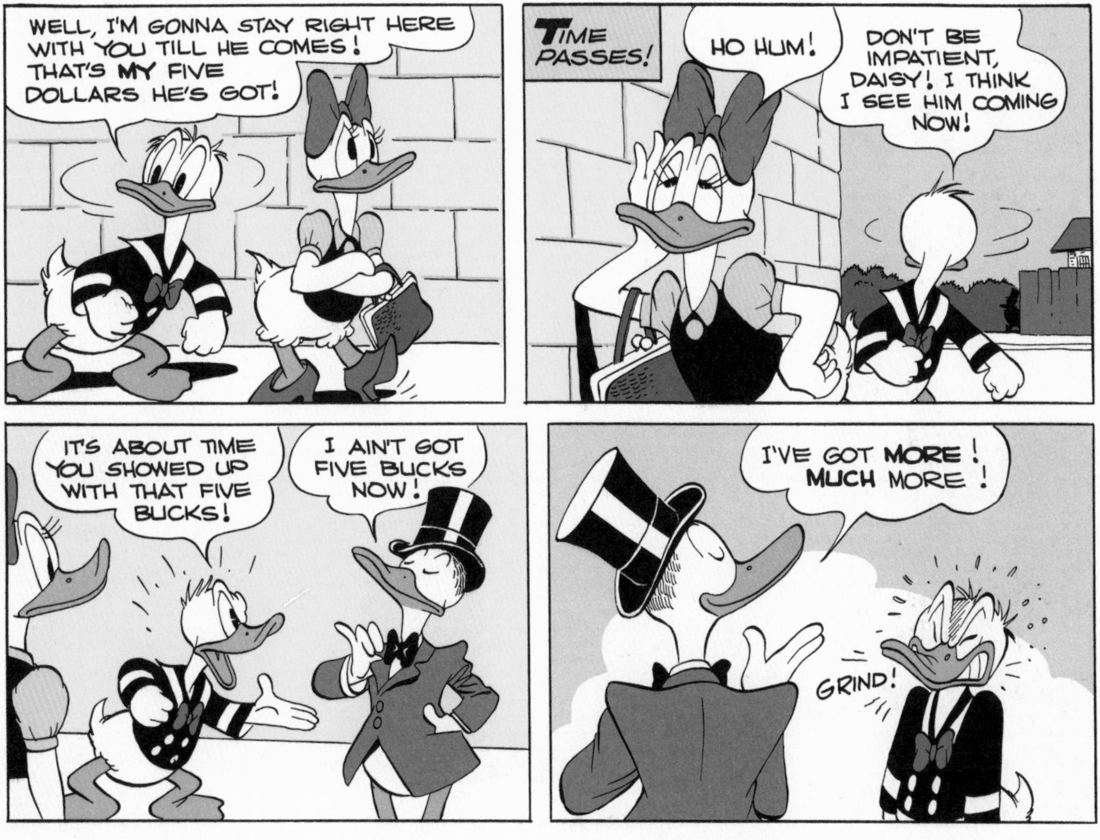
WELL, I'M GONNA STAY RIGHT HERE WITH YOU TILL HE COMES! THAT'S **MY** FIVE DOLLARS HE'S GOT!
TIME PASSES!
HO HUM!
DON'T BE IMPATIENT, DAISY! I THINK I SEE HIM COMING NOW!
IT'S ABOUT TIME YOU SHOWED UP WITH THAT FIVE BUCKS!
I AIN'T GOT FIVE BUCKS NOW!
I'VE GOT **MORE**! **MUCH** MORE!
GRIND!

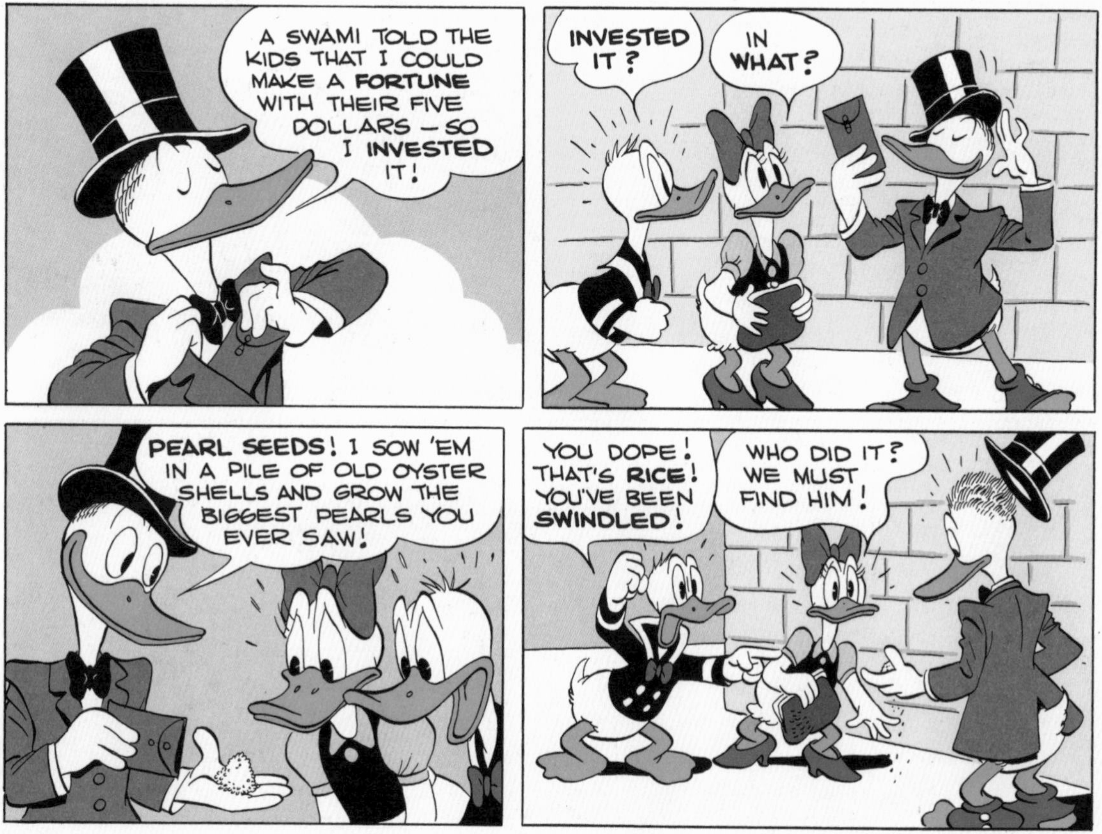
A SWAMI TOLD THE KIDS THAT I COULD MAKE A FORTUNE WITH THEIR FIVE DOLLARS — SO I INVESTED IT!
INVESTED IT?
IN WHAT?
PEARL SEEDS! I SOW 'EM IN A PILE OF OLD OYSTER SHELLS AND GROW THE BIGGEST PEARLS YOU EVER SAW!
YOU DOPE! THAT'S RICE! YOU'VE BEEN SWINDLED!
WHO DID IT? WE MUST FIND HIM!

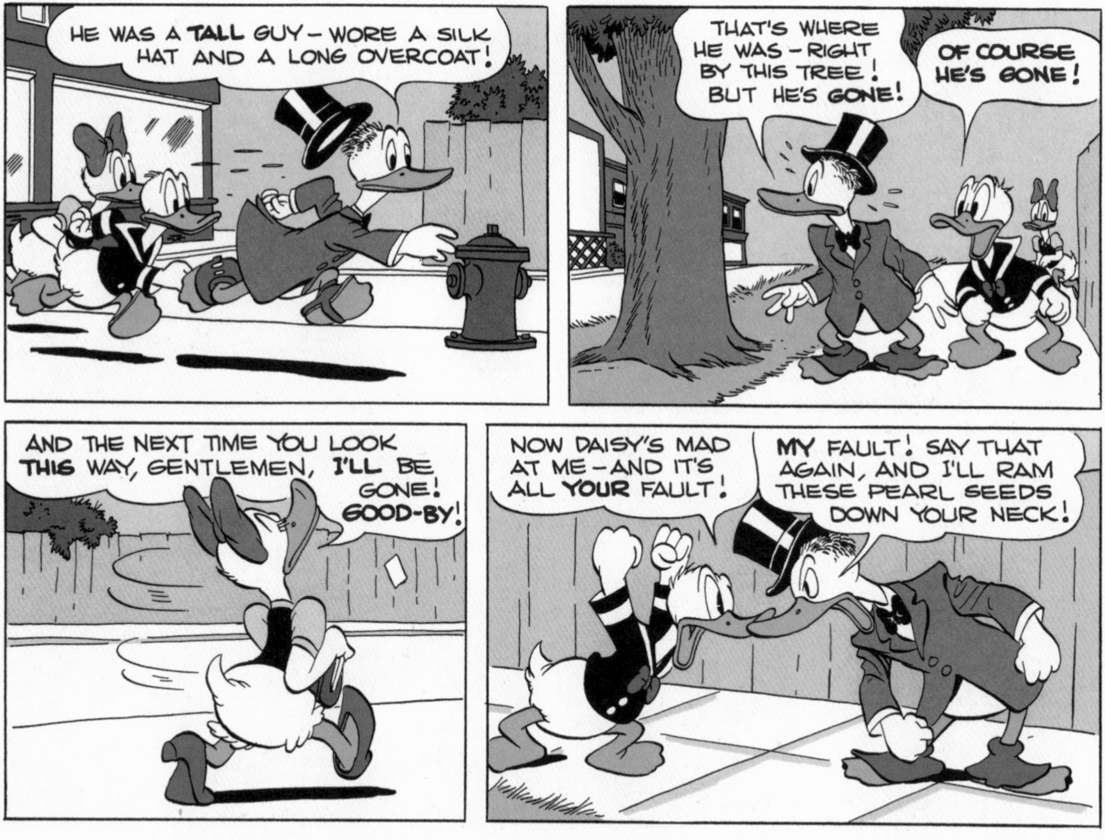
HE WAS A **TALL** GUY—WORE A SILK HAT AND A LONG OVERCOAT!
THAT'S WHERE HE WAS—RIGHT BY THIS TREE! BUT HE'S **GONE**!
OF COURSE HE'S GONE!
AND THE NEXT TIME YOU LOOK **THIS** WAY, GENTLEMEN, **I'LL** BE GONE! **GOOD-BY**!
NOW DAISY'S MAD AT ME—AND IT'S ALL **YOUR** FAULT!
MY FAULT! SAY THAT AGAIN, AND I'LL RAM THESE PEARL SEEDS DOWN YOUR NECK!

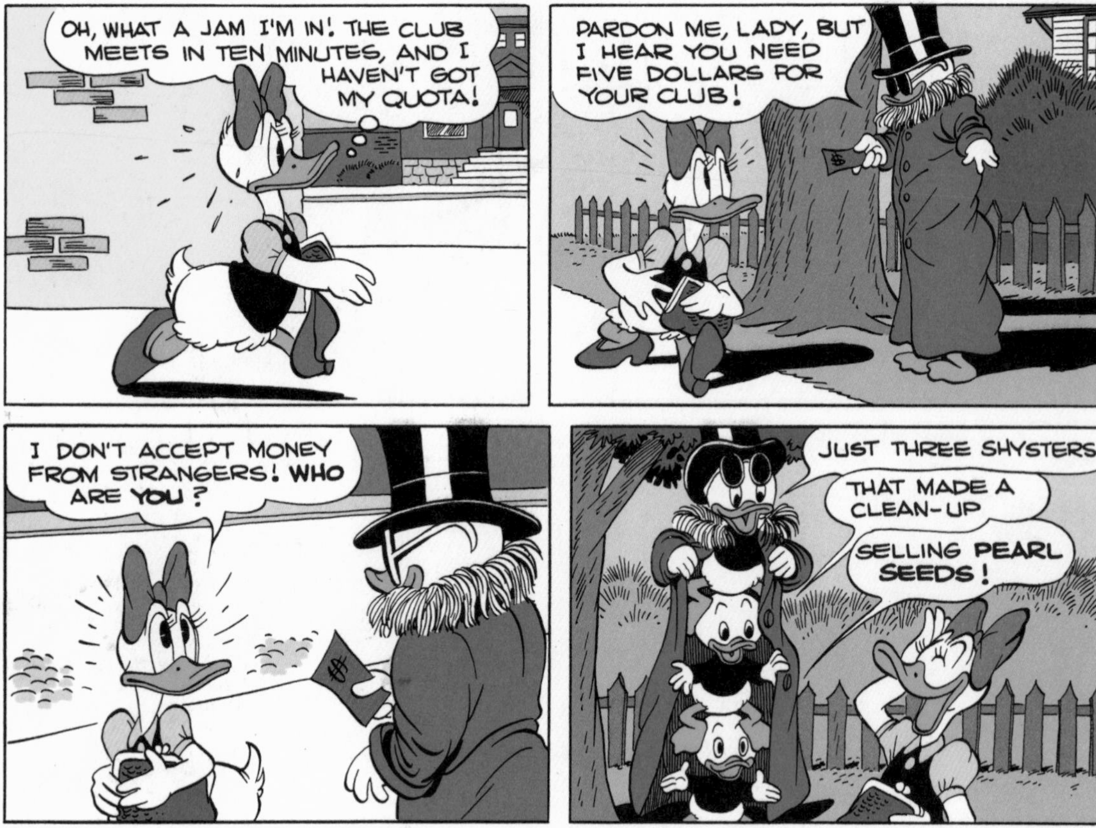
OH, WHAT A JAM I'M IN! THE CLUB MEETS IN TEN MINUTES, AND I HAVEN'T GOT MY QUOTA!
PARDON ME, LADY, BUT I HEAR YOU NEED FIVE DOLLARS FOR YOUR CLUB!
I DON'T ACCEPT MONEY FROM STRANGERS! WHO ARE YOU ?
JUST THREE SHYSTERS
THAT MADE A CLEAN-UP
SELLING PEARL SEEDS!

THE END

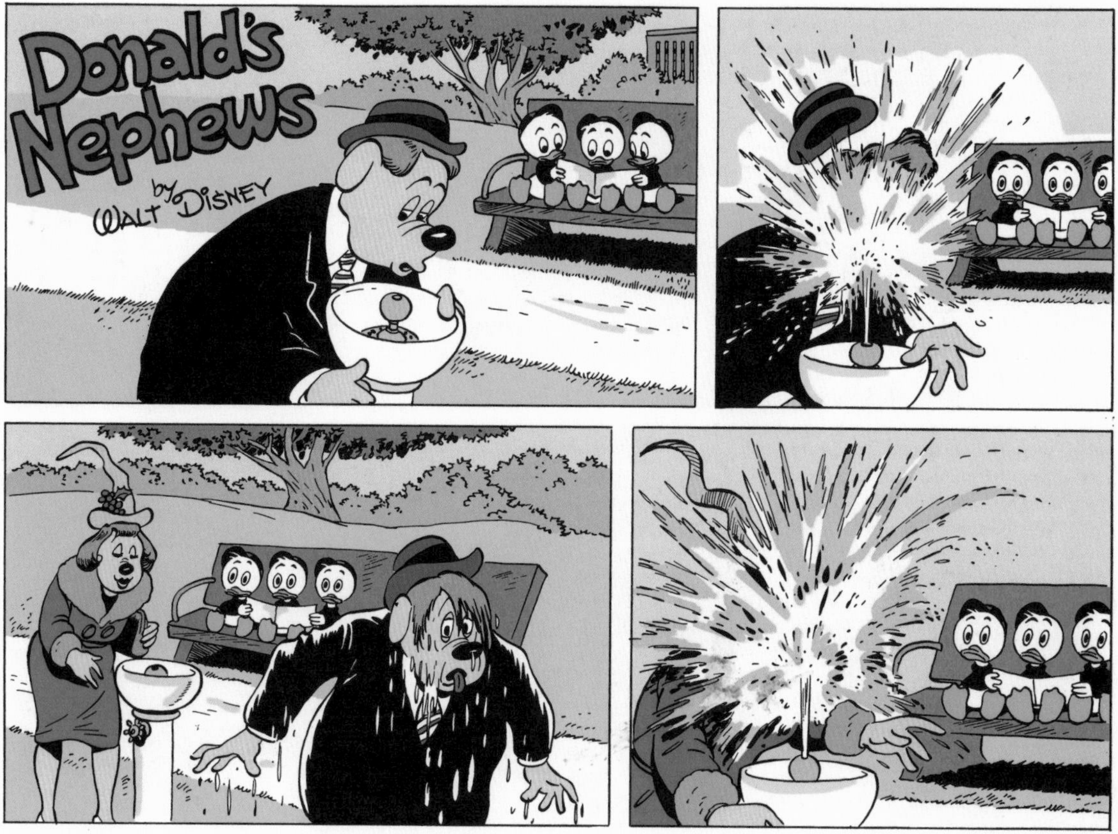
Donald's Nephews
by Walt Disney

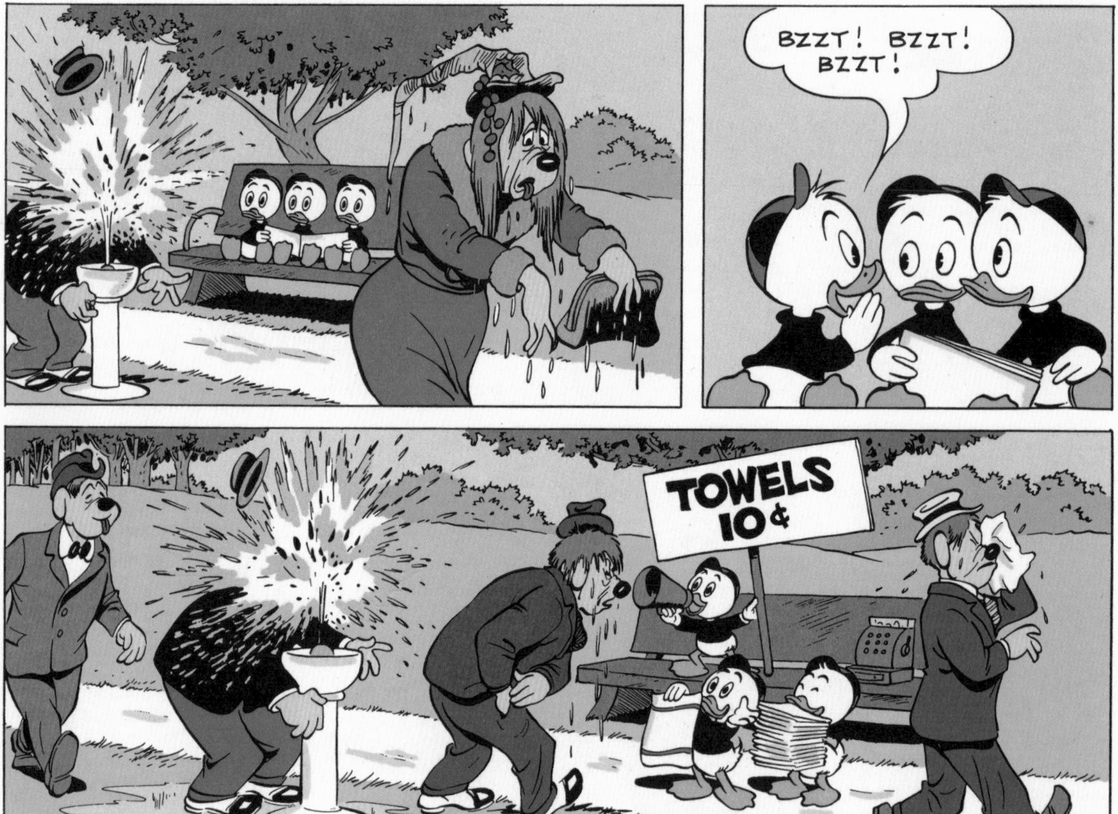
BZZT! BZZT! BZZT!
TOWELS 10¢

THE END